THE MARAUDER

Was it my imagination, or was I getting colder?

A shadow seemed to be blocking out a disc of stars; it was getting larger, closer...

Then I saw it.

Rather, I saw its silhouette. It had moved over the horizon line and was gliding across the brilliant blue-green of the planet below.

It reflected no light; it was as black as the deepest space between the stars. Yet its outline revealed that it was no stray asteroid. Its contours were irregular, and yet *created*.

That's what made my scalp tingle: the strange object below, still on a collision course with my tug, was a *made* object—*but not man-made*. I knew it with an instinct far deeper than science or learning, the way a dog will recognize another dog as one of its own kind, but not a cat...

It was alien.

TED WHITE
Secret of the MARAUDER SATELLITE

A BERKLEY BOOK
published by
BERKLEY PUBLISHING CORPORATION

Copyright © 1968, 1978, by Ted White

All rights reserved

Published by arrangement with the author

All rights reserved which includes the right
to reproduce this book or portions thereof in
any form whatsoever. For information address

Berkley Publishing Corporation
200 Madison Avenue
New York, N.Y. 10016

SBN 425-03888-2

*BERKLEY MEDALLION BOOKS are published by
Berkley Publishing Corporation
200 Madison Avenue
New York, N.Y. 10016*

BERKLEY MEDALLION BOOK® TM 757,375

Printed in the United States of America

Berkley Edition, NOVEMBER, 1978

For Mary, for having inspired
the book...

For Dr. John Boardman, for his
scientific assistance...

And for Robin, for being my wife

Introduction to This Edition

I WROTE THIS BOOK IN 1965. For a book of this nature—
"hard science" fiction, set in the near future (1984)—
that's a risky procedure.

Time *has* tripped me up on a few details. The protagonist says in the first chapter, "I was born in 1966....1966 is the year we lost our first space team." I was off by only a month or two there. Fire at the launching site took our first space team early in 1967. And, "We put our first men on the moon in 1972." I was too conservative: Apollo 11 put our first men on the moon in the summer of 1969.

But in the latter half of the 1970's these are minor points indeed—and it's disturbing to realize that many people might read this book without realizing that either date was incorrect. What has *happened* to our space program?

A fan of science fiction since I was eight years old, I was seduced into this life-long relationship by Robert A. Heinlein's "juvenile" sf novels, starting with the first, *Rocketship Galileo*, which I encountered in the local library shortly after its publication in 1947. I became a science fiction *fan*—someone who writes for and publishes "fanzines" and attends sf conventions—in my early teens and by 1962 I was writing and selling the stuff professionally. The next year I became an editor (at *The*

Magazine of Fantasy & Science Fiction, for which I read unsolicited manuscripts by the trunkload), and the year after that my first sf novel was published.

One day in early 1965 I had a phone call from Henry Morrison. I'd known Henry for many years. We'd both contributed to the same fanzine in the early 1950's, and in 1963 I'd worked briefly for the Scott Meredith Literary Agency (an agency through which a surprisingly large number of sf writers have passed as employees—a sort of Rite of Passage) of which Henry was then vice president. Now Henry was setting up his own agency and he'd seen one of my first paperback novels. He called me up with two proposals. One was that I consider him as my agent (I had no agent then). The other was that I consider writing a "juvenile"—a sf novel written for the teenage market, like those Heinlein novels I'd enjoyed so much.

I had not up to then considered the idea. I'd been writing action-adventure sf—fast-paced stuff with a minimum of dialogue and characterization. But Henry said he thought I could do it, and he pointed out that such books tended to stay in print a long time, earning continuing royalties in the process. (The paperbacks I'd been writing paid a small advance and royalties were a joke.)

After due consideration I took him up on both proposals—and have never regretted it.

The "juvenile" novel is a bastard sort of thing. It is a marketing category more than anything else. It is published for and sold to librarians. The intended readers are teenagers. I have never met a teenaged sf reader who wasn't reading fully "adult" science fiction by that point. The only discernible difference between a "juvenile" sf novel and an "adult" sf novel seems to be the absence of explicit sex and related themes from the "juvenile." A number of Heinlein's "juvenile" sf novels—*Star Beast; Have Spacesuit, Must Travel; Starship Troopers*—were serialized in adult sf magazines and were well received by that audience. At best, then, "juvenile" sf novels were as good as "adult" sf novels, but somewhat restricted in nature.

I knew this, of course, in 1965. I saw the project of writing my own "juvenile" sf novel as an interesting challenge.

I used Heinlein as my model. I analyzed his "juvenile" novels for the elements which had appealed to me and which had made them successful. It seemed to me that Heinlein had adroitly balanced a "hard-science" approach—at times quite didactic—with a mystical appreciation for the wonders of the universe in its vastness. In most of his "juveniles" the immediate plot problems are counterbalanced by a touch of unexplainable alien mystery. I liked that.

The "space station" novel was also an old standby in the field. Heinlein had only touched on what a space station would be and how people would live on one, but del Rey, Leinster and others had devoted whole books to the subject in the early 1950's. Times had changed, and I was aware that many problems had not been foreseen or dealt with. I wanted to do a "space station" book, then. I did some reading on the subject and discovered that there existed a rare breed of radio "ham" who monitored broadcasts from space—from the trial shots going up from both our country and Russia. And these hams were reasonably certain that they'd monitored distress calls from Russian orbital missions. It was fairly likely that some of the Russian Cosmonauts had perished in orbit and remained there, entombed in their capsules.

The assumption was that the Russians had suffered technical failures (they didn't wear space suits), but I considered the possibility that other—alien—causes had been at work. And that gave me my basic plot for the book: the marauder satellite.

The rest of the book came to me almost effortlessly, as I wrote it. And it took me only about three weeks to write the complete novel. The character of the protagonist, Paul Williams—whose name I borrowed from my friend, Paul Williams, the founder of *Crawdaddy* and rock journalism, and then still a sf fan—took shape as I began to write the first chapter and grew steadily until Paul and his problems began to overwhelm the original plot of the book. (In this respect I'm a little unhappy with the way I ended the book—I should have resolved Paul's problems a little more in step with the resolution of the basic plot. However...)

The book was published by a Philadelphia firm, Westminster Press, in 1967. It was an immediate success. Virginia Kirkus and *The Library Journal* loved it. The New York Public Library made it one of their books of the year. It was glowingly reviewed in *Analog* and *Fantasy & Science Fiction* (the reviewer for *Galaxy* managed to "lose" two copies rather than read it and discover his preconceptions about me as a writer might be wrong). Subsequently the book went into five printings in hardcover.

And it has had a surprisingly wide influence. In 1972 I met a science fiction fan, then a college student, who told me he'd read the book at fourteen and it had impressed him more strongly than anything else he'd read. Science fiction writer Gregory Benford wrote a "juvenile" novel, *Jupiter Project*, which was based on my book for its inspiration and "feel." I appeared on a New York City radio program where I met a group of high school students who had read the book and had perceptive comments to make on it.

I think the success of the novel hinged on two aspects: the nature of the protagonist and his problems, which I think any modern sf reader can identify with; and the "hard-science" approach to the space station and actual work in space, which was perhaps better thought out and detailed in *Marauder Satellite* than in any previous and comparable book. I had a lot of fresh material to work with, the product of our space program's achievements at that point. I also had handy a friend, John Boardman, who taught physics at Brooklyn College and who supplied me with the necessary math. But, basically, I think the success of the book was due to my own approach to it.

It was easy for me to remember how I felt as a teenager, easy to approach the protagonist without condescension. I did not "write down" to my audience. I wanted a book which could be read by anyone, of any age, with pleasure—not a book indefinably stamped "kids only."

I wish I could say that the publication of *Marauder Satellite* launched me on a successful new career as a writer, but it did not. I continued to write paperback originals (of, I like to think, increasing quality). In 1968 I became the editor of *Amazing Stories* and its sister publication, *Fantastic Stories,* which I continue to edit today. I wrote two more "juvenile" sf novels. *No Time Like Tomorrow* was published by Crown and was a modest success—not on the same level as *Marauder Satellite*, but the royalty checks have continued to come in steadily over the years. *Trouble on Project Ceres*, for Westminster, was an indirect sequel to this book—set in the same "universe" a few years later, but sharing none of the characters—but suffered at the hands of a new editor who summarily (and over my strongest protests) cut the first two chapters of the book. It got lukewarm reviews in the publications aimed at librarians and sold very poorly. I remain convinced that the loss of those first two chapters was the cause of its lack of commercial success, and the editor remains convinced that she was right and the poor sales were sheer coincidence.

Whichever of us was right, I was so disheartened by my treatment at Westminster that I shelved my plans for future books in the "series"—a very loosely conceived series of books which would form a "future history" of sorts, all growing out of the impact of the alien "marauder satellite"—and I've not attempted a "juvenile" sf novel since then.

It's a little hard for me to realize, when I reread it, that this book is almost twelve years old. It feels as fresh and as alive as it was when I wrote it. It takes me back to a time when space and our space program was still in the daily news and we'd yet to set foot on the moon, but the prospect was enormously exciting—the vindication of all of those of us who believed in science fiction.

—Ted White, 1977

Secret of the MARAUDER SATELLITE

Chapter 1

I MET MARY the first time when we were on a TV show together. I was seventeen then, and still half a year from graduation. I'd been down to the Cape, but all of my space time was simulated. People say it makes no real difference, the simulators are so advanced these days, but there is a difference. You *know* you're participating in an exercise. Bix, my roommate, tells me that they're thinking of using drugs to complete the illusion and make you think you're really out there, but he's full of wild stories, ideas, and schemes, and I discount them all heavily.

But this TV thing—it's one of those scholastic shows where they parade us, America's Youth, out for a trained-seal act. We compete in teams while they throw questions at us, ranging from "What peninsula is bounded on the west and south by the Atlantic Ocean and on the east by the Mediterranean?" to "What Indianapolis racing driver introduced the first commercially produced front wheel drive to automobiles?" with a wide variety of literature and quantum mechanics thrown in to keep us on our toes.

I was in my first show when I was eleven, and I was proud and scared. We came in second out of three teams, so I felt sort of cheated—neither winner nor loser. But I wanted nothing more to do with the things. They sat you there and threw questions at you, and you felt the whole weight of your teammates, friends, school, parents, everybody—while you struggled against the sinking feeling that you'd lose your mind and your memory and, in one second, against every would-be manly instinct, were going to start crying.

It's worse than Little League Baseball.

I'm a test-wise guy. They've been giving me tests since I learned to read and write, age four. Throughout the first half of grade school, I rebelled. I was what is euphemistically called an "underachiever," meaning that I refused to do better than make passing grades. But by the time I was in fifth grade and things were getting interesting, I was getting interested. Then there was no stopping me. Tests, TV shows, more tests, and then NASA.

The NASA program is a godsend; I don't think I could have taken normal high school. NASA pulled me out of junior high and threw me into five years of the devil's personal torments, designed to crash-program me with high school, college, and grad school training, plus military training, and most important to me and the sole justification for the whole thing, space flight training.

I was a space cadet.

It's something we laughed over, the first year. Shades of old TV reruns—Junior Spacemen of the Space Academy and all that. And, in a very real sense, that's what we were. We were being trained to be the spacemen of tomorrow.

But back to Mary. We'd been tapped to go on the TV show, and despite my bold resolutions of the years past, I went on. We were one of three teams, the other two from the new junior colleges that seem to be catching on these days for the bright kids who want to skip high school.

This is going to sound silly, but I'm scared of those younger kids. I'm nineteen now, and I've had over a year in space, and it's been all I'd bargained for and more. But

I'm scared of those supersmart kids who, without the pressure schooling I've had, are just as smart and probably can outthink me at every turn.

While we train for the glory of country and the future of space, those kids are lining up plush corporate futures of their own, and someday, when I'm retired and an old man in my thirties, one of those bright-types is going to be looking at me from across a desk and saying, "O.K., so you know space. But what can you *do*, Mr. Williams? Where can we fit you into *our* picture?" And I'm not sure I'll have the answer.

I was the oldest on the show; my teammates were both sixteen. And the other teams averaged sixteen in age. Mary was fifteen.

There was nothing special about her that I remember. She wore glasses, and had long hair done up in a bun. I remember noticing during the preshow warm-up that she was rather tall for a girl, but I was tense—we were all tense—and I wasn't noticing much about the competition. I was spending my time preparing myself for the ordeal by blanking out my surroundings and telling myself, "This is just another test, kid. You've been taking tests—written tests, oral tests, all kinds—for years. Don't sweat it." It was like the one play I was in. All the other kids backstage the first night were joking and jittering. I was convinced it was just another dress rehearsal, and utterly cool about the whole bit. It wasn't until the *second* night that I had my stage fright.

We came in second again, a very close second. Mary's team beat us by ten points, which is the closest margin possible. The third team was eighty points behind, and I remember a rather pinch-faced girl on that team stamping angrily on the floor, her face screwed up as if she was going to throw a tantrum any moment. That's what I hate about these shows. I'd noticed her before the show, and she was one of these compulsively lively types, very outgoing, very cheerful. Now she was totally shot down. People have no right to do that to us.

Mary, on the other hand, was radiant, in a quiet sort of way. There was a party afterward, awkwardly informal, where we sipped Pepsis and watched the adults with their cigarettes and cocktails and wondered where the dividing line was. The moderator of the show had a fine speaking voice and an I.Q. of not over 120.

I congratulated Mary on her team's win, and said, "Mary Cramer—your father isn't Maxfield Cramer, is he?"

"Well, as a matter of fact, he is."

"How about that," I said. "We had him for a seminar last year. He's up there now, isn't he?" Maxfield Cramer is a space scientist. That's an inexact label, but the labeling process in the scientific fields has been breaking down now for years. Cramer had been an astronomer and a biologist. He'd gone up to the Station to do research on space-traveling spores, and to establish the first space-mounted observatory. He'd ended up with a finger in every pie he could find. For him it was a lifetime's dream come true.

I can't kid myself I'll ever be a science man. I'll go into space, and I'll make a good spaceman—I may even become an astronaut—but I'm practically oriented. I'm a doer, not a thinker, when it comes right down to it.

So we said a few more polite things to each other, Mary agreeing that her father was now back up at the Station, and mentioning what a tense grind the show was, and like that. I thought she was rather pretty, rather a nice girl, but in the NASA academy you don't have enough free time to get seriously concerned about girls, and somehow I never missed it. But it did strike me at the time that she was, in addition to being an attractive kid, one smart one as well. And I've always laid my plans for marriage upon the solid foundation of intelligence plus beauty. As I've said to Bix, "What's a pretty object, if you can't talk to it now and then?" to which he has nodded sagely and added, "I trust you want more than just to talk to an attractive slide rule," and then we have started discussing emotional maturity index factors, and that is a long digression. At any rate, I filed Mary Cramer away in my mind to be considered as possible wife material, come marrying time. And since that looked to be some distance away yet, I filed her pretty far back.

I haven't been too careful with my details so far—Bix says that I have an inherently disordered mind; I'm always digressing on my digressions—so let me fill you in a bit.

I was born in 1966. I used to take a lot of kidding about how unlucky that is for a spaceman—1966 is the year we lost our first space team. But even at that, they were wrong: I was lucky.

We put our first men on the moon in 1972. I remember the tremendous hullabulloo on TV—they'd interrupted *Capt. Whizz and His Intergalactic Patrol* to broadcast all these terribly dull scenes of men sitting around talking to each other and looking at monitors, and every so often announcing something or other.

By 1978 we had the primary wheel of the space station in orbit. It was staffed entirely by the military by then, but NASA had already taken the space program out of the hands of the military, and the new training program was five years under way.

There are two good reasons for training your spaceman early and using him while he's young. The first reason is the one that's been a cliché in science fiction for the last three decades: a man is at his physical prime between ages fifteen and twenty-five, centering between eighteen and twenty-one. He'll never again have such finely toned reflexes, either physical or mental. And for all the computers they've put into orbit, we've had to depend time and again on human reflex. The second reason is one they didn't discover until they started orbiting men: Prolonged weightlessness in older men produces something they call hypotension. Basically, the older you are, the harder time you have readjusting to standard gravity after being weightless, say, for two weeks or longer. Your heart and circulatory system find it easy to take weightlessness—much easier—but the older you are, the less easy it is to go back to full-time work again.

This doesn't matter for a lot up in the tin can, of course, where one G is maintained on the rims. But an active spaceman may spend a lot of time up there when he's not on the rim, or even in the Station itself. And he's got to be able to take the transitions.

So they grab 'em young. They grabbed me young. When I was twelve I was popped into the NASA training academy—usually referred to as the Space School—and given five years of intensive schooling and training, rarely with any time off for good behavior.

I graduated just before I turned eighteen. I'd had all they could give me—and about all I could take of them. I was as prepared for space as I'd ever be. So, in 1984, they shipped me up to my brave new world: space.

We were flown east to New York City first. We were getting a three-day stopover: a chance for one last wild fling before departure. I'm sure I don't know what they expected. I'm not one for sight-seeing, so I decided I'd ride the subways, peering out of the front window in the first car. That had been one of my favorite pastimes in Chicago and the Bay Area.

They put us in a quiet hotel, just east of Central Park. I had my own room, which was no great difference to me, since I wasn't that close to any of the guys along on the trip anyway. There were seven of us, and neither of the close friends I'd made in school had graduated yet. I was left with guys who had their own friendships and cliques, of which I was no part.

It occurs to me that I haven't actually described myself. I suppose this is because I take myself for granted, having lived with me for a good number of years—most of my life, actually—and my mental image of myself doesn't match up too closely with what a stranger might make of me.

I'm a little short—five feet eleven inches—and stocky. I have dirty blond hair, the kind which is just nondescript enough that no one is quite sure whether to call it blond or brown. I've been shaving since I was fourteen, but it wouldn't matter if I didn't; my beard is all but invisible. This used to bother me, but it doesn't anymore. Sometimes I skip days between shaves. I was one of those who matured early. I remember in the gym, getting pinned on the wrestling mat and hearing somebody say, "Hey, what ugly hairy legs." I threw the guy I was wrestling. And I went through pimples two years before my classmates, to my early unhappiness and later glee.

What else? I like to think of myself as hard-bitten, a realist. Practical, the sort to order his life. Bix tells me that this is purest baloney; that I am an incurable dreamer, always messy, and blessed with a cluttered, disorderly mind. Take your pick. From the way this is going, I'd say Bix is closer to the truth. But I'll get to Bix later, if I can ever untangle my chronology and tell this story right.

Meeting Mary again seemed at first the purest coincidence.

I'd wandered down to the lobby, after shaking off Mr. Farnsworth, one of our chaperons, telling him I just wanted to wander over to the park and get a little sun.

"Watch yourself, Paul," he said. "That park has a bad reputation." I told him I thought I could handle myself—I'd had Marine training in self-defense, after all—and left him standing by the elevator with his mouth open as the doors closed. You'd think that if you were old enough to risk your life in space, you might be trusted to behave intelligently in New York City. (Bix tells me that it was only the government's investment in me that Farnsworth was safeguarding.)

When I went over to the lobby candy counter to buy peanuts for squirrel-feeding, I heard somebody call behind me. I turned around.

And there was this girl. She was slender, sort of leggy, actually, with long hair that curled down over her shoulders. She wore glasses, and a smile. The smile was what did it: I remembered that smile.

"Hi," she said. "Remember me?"

"Mary Cramer," I said. "Star of stage, screen, and TV. How could I forget you? You outscored me."

"I heard you were staying here," she said. "Are you going down to the Cape from here?"

"Thursday," I said. "We've got three days' leave to enjoy ourselves in the Big City."

"Have you made any plans?" she asked.

"Not really." I wondered what all this was leading up to.

"Daddy is staying here," she said. "How would you like to have dinner with us?"

Now you'll have to take this on faith, but the prospect of dinner with Maxfield Cramer was a good deal more interesting to me than Mary was. Cramer was one of those men like the legendary Von Braun; there'd been a time in the not very distant past when I'd worshiped him. Mary — well, Mary was a pretty seventeen-year-old, and smart, and entered in my file of future wife material, but at this moment no great attraction to me.

So I was mostly being polite and returning invitation for invitation when, after I accepted hers, I said, "I'm going across the street to the park. Want to come along?"

"Sure," she said. "Why not?" She noticed the bag of peanuts. "Going to feed the squirrels? Those are the salted kind. You'd have much better luck with the kind that have shells."

"If the squirrels don't care for them," I said, "I'll eat them myself." I was wondering why I was feeling vaguely irritated. And why I hadn't thought about the difference in peanuts myself.

The street was full of sunshine, flapping pigeons, and cars. It was a pleasant day, and one, I'm told, that was typical of the city. A vague mist seemed to hang in the sky, so that the sunshine was yellower, and when you look down a long avenue, the more distant buildings become progressively lighter shades of gray. There's a smell to these days, too, although I can't quite pin it down. Sort of like the seashore; not a waterfront smell, but yet the smell of water. Right now, where I'm writing this, I'm breathing canned, recycled air, and despite all attempts, it smells of too many people closed in among themselves, and it carries the sharpness of ozone and air-freshening scents. And that peculiar, far-off smell of New York City—sort of cool, salty, and humid, blended with the smell of trees and freshmown grass in the park—makes me feel a sad tingle of homesickness, despite everything.

We crossed over into the park and followed one of the winding paths past baseball fields, flower gardens, a lake with people rowing on it, and up a series of hills. Finally we stopped, pausing to rest on a park bench in a secluded copse of trees. The path forked as it rose up for the next hill, and an outcropping of rock sat in the center of the fork, with an old gnarled tree growing over it and stretching out over us. I opened my bag of peanuts.

A squirrel scampered down the tree and out onto the rock overlooking us. It rose up and clutched a forepaw to its breast. It looked very plaintive and sad; less a beggar than someone desperately in need but too proud to seek charity. "Hey, there," I said, and held out a peanut in my hand.

I've since learned that the squirrels in Central Park have their humans so perfectly trained that whether or not you have anything, you will automatically make the gesture of offering something to the little beasts. And you'll feel guilty if your hand is empty.

The squirrel jumped down to the walk and scampered closer, in a sort of sidewise, skittish motion. I flipped my peanut out at it. The squirrel jumped back, then eagerly forward, to snatch at the peanut, and then made a great leap with it back to the edge of the rock.

I never got to find out whether it liked salted peanuts.

That backward leap was the tip-off—we'd been so

engrossed in the squirrel that we'd been oblivious to the approach of strangers. I looked up.

There were five of them in immediate sight, and I had no idea if there were more. They all looked to be my age or younger, but there's where the resemblance stopped.

I made it a point to find out about these types afterward, and I was told that they were "an unfortunate product of urban conditions." What that means is, they are what happens when you overcrowd a city, hike the rents way up, put half the families on welfare, and then start shuttling them from slum to slum in the name of urban renewal—which always somehow seems to accommodate fewer people than it dispossesses. I know a guy up here in the Station who is one of the aerospace military team. He comes from Harlem, but I don't hold that against him. He told me he was born in a tenement where he shared two rooms with his family of eight and a population of rats at least equal in number. Theoretically at least, he could've been one of those guys in the park—for all I know, maybe one of his brothers was—but he pulled himself out of it. Why? I don't know. It doesn't seem right to say that some people are born bad, but at the same time I can't quite go along with those social-worker types who want to blame everything on everyone else but the kid himself. There's got to be an answer somewhere in between, but I haven't got it. Neither, I suspect, has anyone else.

Anyway, to put it in plain language, these guys who were ringing us were members of a gang—kid gangsters, really—which made Central Park a cruising ground. They were looking for what trouble they could find, and right now we were It.

"Hey, looka blondy, feedin' the squirrels," said one of them with a sneer.

"Hey, don't stop just 'cause we're here," said a short little guy with a bandanna tied around his head.

"Yeah, we like to feed the squirrels," the first one said. With a sort of negligent move he batted the bag of peanuts from my hand, and they spilled on the ground.

I didn't do anything. I didn't want to start any real trouble, not with Mary there. And I am very realistic about myself. I can handle myself pretty nicely, but against five—very likely carrying knives? Bad odds. So I sat there and took it.

"Hey, you spilled your peanuts," the leader said. "Better pick them up before somebody walks on 'em."

"That's all right," I said quietly.

"Hey, what'd I say? Pick 'em up, buddy."

"Let the squirrels have them," I said.

He cuffed me against the back of my neck, driving me off the bench and onto my knees. *"Pick them up,"* he repeated. He clubbed me on the back of my neck again. "With your mouth, buddy. Just like a squirrel."

Well, there's a limit. I mean, I didn't think it would matter to him that squirrels usually use their forepaws—their hands—to pick things up. And I'd been pushed about as far as I could let myself go. Mary still worried me, though. If I started something, well, she was just a girl, and I didn't like to think about it.

So I hesitated, and the guy started to kick at me.

Mary let out a good, healthy scream. It was loud.

I grabbed the foot that was aimed at me and stood up, twisting. The guy landed on his face in the dust.

The next three seconds were kaleidoscopic. One of them jumped me, getting on my back and trying to choke me with his arm around my neck. I threw him. Then I heard a thin, high-pitched scream, and saw another one clutching his arm, which was sticking out at the wrong angle. He was backing away from Mary.

Then, simultaneously it seemed, there were police whistles, and the area was empty, except for us.

Chapter 2

NATURALLY, THAT WASN'T the end of it.

The next three hours were punctuated by lectures. The first lecture was from a police sergeant, who asked me what I thought I was doing, "bringing a nice girl into a park like this." You could see he had his own ideas. If you ask me, he was a lot more interested in scaring honest citizens out of the park than he was in making it safe for them.

Then there was Mr. Farnsworth, who was absolutely shocked that I would expose Mary to "that sort of thing."

"Well, I don't know," I said. "She took pretty good care of herself." It was very illuminating to discover that Mary knew karate.

"Young man," Mr. Farnsworth said, his face as livid as raw liver, "that is exactly the sort of flippant remark I would expect of you. You seem to have absolutely no awareness of anyone but yourself. You seem to feel that by having escaped the serious consequences of your foolishness that you are above reproach. I would like to ask you just one question: Did you know beforehand that Miss Cramer could defend herself against such an attack?"

"No, sir," I said.

"Very well," he nodded. "I trust I have made my point."

Win one, lose one.

"Conditions aren't good here in the East, Paul," Dr. Cramer told me. I sawed at my meat and kept my mouth shut. This man was not another Farnsworth.

Dr. Cramer had a face like that of your friendly neighborhood pharmacist: wise and twinkling eyes, which seemed to crinkle every time he laughed; a firm jaw getting just a little jowly, strong flat-planed cheeks, and a receding hairline behind which the hair was as dark as Mary's. I was having dinner with Mary and her father. Each of us struggled not to say what we each privately thought about the hotel's room-service fare.

"The jet streams have been changing their patterns erratically for over twenty years now—that's one of the weather situations we've been studying up on the Station—and the results are right at hand. They've been having five-year drought cycles all over the eastern part of the country for a full generation. Think about that, Paul."

I thought about it. "You mean the farm disaster programs, sir? But the East doesn't grow much these days, and the Midwest has been getting along all right. I mean, there's no crush on food—we're still feeding half of Asia on our surpluses. The eastern farms were mostly two-bit farms to start out with."

"Yes, they were. And they didn't lend themselves to amalgamation—to corporate ownership. So they were run by families, Paul. And while we don't need their food, *they* do. Every time the government buys a wiped-out farm, Paul, the people leave. They're leaving homes that may have been in the family for generations. They're leaving a drought-devastated battlefield, with charity money in their pockets, and little prospects for a new career. Most of those families will end up in the big cities, on welfare. Most of the men will be embittered, just as the coal miners in the Appalachia region were in the previous generation. They've lost their homes, and more important, the dignity of work. They will be on the dole for the rest of their lives."

"Oh, now, come on," I said. "That's too much. There are new jobs opening up every day—plenty of retraining programs. There's plenty of work!"

"Sure—for trained technicians, for men with skills. You're a very young man, Paul. Life is still opening up for you, and you've trained for a forward-looking career. But—let's just suppose that next week the government voted to close down the space program. What then?"

"Huh? They wouldn't do that. That's ridiculous!"

"Is it? The government has spent more money on the space effort now than it has for every war effort of this century. Did you know that? Every year, Congress budgets billions for the continuing space program—more than any other single program or department. In three days, Paul, you and I and your classmates will be taking a rocket up from Cape Kennedy, which will eat sizably into that budget, just for its launching and use.

"And so far the space program has not *begun* to pay off in a tangible way. So far it has not returned even pennies on each dollar it swallows up."

"Are you serious, sir? Would they—*could* they close it all down?" For some reason the muscles in my stomach were clenched and knotting, and the roast cardboard on my plate did not even smell appetizing.

"I doubt it. But it's something you should never let entirely out of your thoughts. The space program has not *always* existed—and may not always. So let's play a game. Let's say they close it down. What will you do?"

"I—I don't know." I found myself chewing on my underlip. "I guess I've never thought about it—until now." It was a thoroughly scary thought, I can tell you. Five years' training—five years of *intensive* training—all pointed toward that single goal. Five years—more than a quarter, almost a third of my life—and pretty much the whole of my thinking (*adult*, as I thought of it to myself; after all, I was biologically adult at twelve, wasn't

I?) life. All directed toward that single goal.

Dr. Cramer was just playing a game, he said. But I could see what he was driving at, plainly enough. *What would I do, if I couldn't go into space?* My stomach felt as if I was in free fall.

"I—I see what you mean, sir."

"But you're young," he said, hammering the point home. "You could retrain easily; your whole adult life is ahead of you." There it was again—that casual adult assumption that Life Begins at Eighteen.

"O.K.," he said, smiling. "So back to my original point. I don't have the statistics, but hundreds of farms are failing every year. The ones that made it through the previous drought cycles have been sucked dry. And every day new families—dislocated, embittered, stripped of their dignity—come to the cities, including this one.

"They're coming from the North, from upstate, and from the South. They're restless, and they're worried, and they're fair prey for every sharpie in the city. They're shoved off into ghettos, charged every cent of their welfare checks for the rent of apartments that were substandard forty years ago—and nobody knows what to do with them.

"This city is just one big pressure kettle, Paul, and somebody forgot to include the safety valve. It's in a state of crisis now, and it's heading for a showdown. I don't want to be here when that happens. Tempers are already too short."

"It's so hard to realize," Mary said quietly. She'd stayed out of it, so far, but I knew that she was on my side—she didn't blame me for what had happened in the park. And let's face it—I'm not that stupid—neither did Dr. Cramer. He hadn't been chewing me out; he'd been *explaining*, filling me in, giving me the data.

He smiled at his daughter. "It is, and I don't blame either of you. I can look out of the window of my bedroom here, and watch nurses walking their baby carriages in the park. I can see the kids playing baseball, tennis, rowing on the lake. It couldn't look more peaceful.

"But I'll give you odds that every one of those nurses is armed, if only with a tear-gas pencil. And I saw with my own eyes two baseball teams mixing it up in a real free-for-all with bats and all." He shook his head. "Took the cops fifteen minutes to break it up." He tapped his wristwatch. It was a fine piece of work, two stop hands, and a five-digit calculator. "I timed it myself."

I hadn't had a chance to talk to Mary throughout the afternoon, and she'd been pretty quiet, almost subdued, I thought. It was bothering me; I'd had some idea of what I'd gotten her into—and a pretty good notion of how it might've turned out if we hadn't been quite so lucky.

Let me put it straight: I didn't like Farnsworth one bit, but I had to admit he was right. He'd warned me in the first place, and I was too cocky to pay any attention to him. Then I compounded my error by taking a girl—a *girl!*—into the park.

I don't like to be wrong—that's fundamental. I never have. It hurts when I'm wrong in front of my friends, but it's a lot worse when I'm wrong before those I dislike. Bix says that it's a simple case of an antisocial attitude coupled with a superiority complex. Bix has a lot of answers, though.

But what came through on top of this was the vague naggings of something I haven't often felt: my conscience. It'd been so long since I'd had to answer for anyone but myself that it took me a while to realize just what was really bothering me.

I'd been *responsible* for Mary when she accompanied me to the park—let alone the fact that she was both smarter and better able to defend herself; she was a *girl*. I was responsible. I'd shirked that responsibility. Dr. Cramer talked all the way around it; he's subtle. He just reminded me of how everyone else had forfeited *his* responsibility.

After dinner Dr. Cramer excused himself and left the

room, and Mary and I were alone. It was the first time since we'd been in the park. I felt suddenly awkward, ill at ease. I seized the bull by the horns:

"Umm, Mary, I guess you've got an apology coming." I could feel my face getting hot.

She was quiet for a moment, as though figuring out what her response should be. "For what?"

"It was a pretty stupid stunt I pulled—" I began.

"You're being brainwashed!" she interrupted.

"Huh?"

"So, O.K.," she said, "we got mixed up in something. But who started it? The way everybody has been acting, you'd think we went into that park looking for trouble! You know that's not so." She looked up at me and our eyes locked for a moment. "You don't owe me any apologies, Paul. Maybe we should've known better than to walk into an attractive public park in broad daylight"—her tone was scathingly sarcastic for a moment—"but the only thing we were guilty of was simple ignorance, and that was as much mine as yours. And when it comes right down to it, you did a pretty good job on those punks." A sudden grin flashed across her face. "Besides—it was fun."

I felt as if a load had just disappeared from my shoulders, and my back straightened. "Yeah?"

"Those poor guys—I bet they never knew what hit them!" She giggled.

Talk about responsibility!

"I never had a chance to try it out before," she said. "My karate training, I mean."

"I never thought anything like that would happen," I said. "But, you know? It's been years since anybody's tried to beat up on me—outside of gym class, I mean." We were both grinning now. We were co-conspirators, buddies tested in combat.

Then I sobered a bit. "It was a pretty lucky thing, though, the way it worked out."

"We *were* lucky," she nodded. "But don't worry

about it now. My father says the time for worrying is when it'll do the most good. Never cry over spilt milk. We were lucky, but we did all right for ourselves. We've got no complaints coming now."

"Yeah, except that I doubt if I'll be able to set one foot out of this hotel again without a chaperon," I said glumly.

"Well," she said, her cheeks dimpling with another grin, "*that's* worth worrying about."

I was right, of course: I wasn't allowed out of the hotel for the rest of our stay in New York City. But in a way, that was a good thing. That's how I came to know Bix.

I mentioned, I think, that I didn't really know the other seven in my group very well. We knew each other to nod to, but that was about it. Enforced contact soon put an end to that.

With my usual incomplete grasp of interpersonal relationships, I'd assumed they were all buddy-buddy—a big happy group that excluded me. They weren't, of course, although for the moment they had a common bond which did exclude me: they were all pretty burned with me.

It was my fault. I had Abused My Privileges, so all of us were under close watch—which is to say, we were all on leash because of my incident in the park.

"I guess you think you pulled a smart one, Williams?" Bob Krassner had elected himself ringleader. It was a new game, designed to take the edge off their enforced idleness. It was called Bait Paul Williams.

"That's right, Krassner," I told him. "I did it just for you."

"How's that, fella?" he asked, snapping the bait. I was trying out a new game of my own.

"Why, I know how badly you did in Applied Defense, old buddy," I said, "and as Mr. Farnsworth says, that park is no place for kids."

He was staring at me, his mouth working a little. I sunk the shaft in the rest of the way: "I knew you'd end up there if they let you do any wandering." I leaned closer, with a conspiratorial air. "I had to play it subtle, you know? If I'd just gone and told Farnsworth, 'Hey, Bobby Krassner's going to get in trouble if you let him out,' well, it would've been embarrassing, you know what I mean? They don't like to admit they couldn't make Trained Killers out of us all."

He was purpling nicely. "So my way, I shoulder the blame, get a chance to try a few tricks, and—with no personal prejudice to your record, fella—I keep you safely out of harm's way." I gave him my most sincere smile. "Don't thank me; I'd do it for anyone."

Ralph Ward and Al Beiderbecke had been standing close by, taking it all in. Beiderbecke was laughing. I turned my back on them all, and headed out of the lounge. I wanted to try the solitary comfort of my room.

"Hey, Williams." It was Beiderbecke, catching up to me. "Good show."

"Your turn now?" I asked him. "Any number can play."

"No beef, Paul," he said, falling into step with me. "Why don't you take the chip off your shoulder? We'll be seeing a lot of each other for quite a spell yet, and where we'll be, there won't be any parks across the street. You know?"

"Ummm. A good point." I paused at the door to the hall. "Going up to my room. Doing anything?" That's the closest I've come to an open invitation for friendship in a long time.

"Around here? You have to be kidding. Sure, let's go."

I looked back over my shoulder. Krassner was pouting at Ward, and they were deep in conversation. I figured he was explaining to Ward how superior he was to me for not descending to my level, and all that. In the back of my mind was the nagging thought that with my penchant for making quick enemies it was maybe not so wise to let myself get cooped up with them in a large tin can for six months. I suppressed it.

Secret of the Marauder Satellite

Alphonse Beiderbecke had a total dislike for his first name, even shortened to Al. One of the first things he told me was that as far as he was concerned, anybody who wanted to consider himself a friend would kindly refrain from ever using the name. "Call me Bix," he said. "It comes to me from a distant and illustrious member of the family." And Bix he was, from then on.

Bix was tall, thin, nervous-looking, and constantly on the move. It made me tired, just to watch him. He is one of the purest examples of ectomorph I have ever seen. He eats like a horse, and he tells me that his weight has never topped one hundred and forty pounds. He stands a little over six feet tall. His hair is black, really black, and so are his eyes. He has a way of cocking his head at you, staring at you intently with those dark eyes, and saying, "You know, Paul, the trouble with you is you're a paranoid."

"Aw, come off it." I do not like to be analyzed, and I haven't, ever since a year and a half of thrice weekly sessions with Dr. Spittal right after I first came to the Space School.

"No, I mean it: you're lucky you're just paranoid."

"I could forget you asked me to call you Bix, you know," I said.

"Last year in school, I helped out with the records in the Psych Department," Bix said quietly.

I could feel myself getting angry.

"You should see the records that are kept in there—case histories on every guy who ever set one foot in the door. I mean, everybody, even the guys who flunked out after one week.

"Let me tell you something, Paul: Every one of those guys—and me, too—we've all got records as thick as your final thesis. They've got us taped, all the way back to our first spank in the delivery room, and how much fuss we made about it.

"So listen to me for a minute. I've got my ambitions—I aim to be a shrink when they cashier me out of space. It's important to have a secondary occupation lined up, you know; something handy to fall back on when you're getting middle-aged. And I've got a healthy curiosity about people. Especially the people I'm going to be stuck with on this first assignment.

"I went through all the records on each of you seven guys, Paul. I had to." His expression was very tense, but he gave me a fleeting smile then. "I think they knew what I was up to; I'm pretty sure Spittal did.

"I was looking for something, Paul. I was looking for someone.

"It's going to be tough up there. We're raw; we're going to be on the spot all the time until we really settle in to our jobs, and it's going to be tense.

"Times like that, everybody needs a friend—a real friend. Somebody he doesn't have to tense up around, somebody he can unlax with."

He was pacing back and forth across the end of the room. Then he stopped and pointed his finger in my direction. "That's why I picked you, Paul. I—I checked out the records on all seven of you, and you were the one."

I stared at him, trying to figure him out.

"So, O.K., you're a paranoid. It's in the records. You're a go-it-aloner, antisocial. But that's no big problem. Paranoia is the easiest thing in the world to shuck, once you realize what you're working with, and make the big decision to get free of it. Now, I figure, with my training—my abilities—to help, you should be able to iron yourself out within a few weeks. It's no big thing to start with, and with my help—what do you say?"

I was still staring at him, and my eyes were burning. This lanky sketch of a male adult human being had dug up my complete psychological case history, run it through his computerlike mind, and decided that with very little trouble he could cure me and be my friend. Just like that.

And you know something?

I believed him.

Chapter 3

THE FLIGHT DOWN to Cape Kennedy was without incident. It was a clear day on the eastern seaboard—well, as clear as it ever gets these days—and the flight was just like the ones I'd been on before, when we'd been given field trips to the Cape.

Except that this was the real thing.

None of us had really done much more than pick at our breakfasts that morning, and there was a strong tension in the air. We were all on edge, and yet there was this brotherhood feeling among us—a shared awareness that whatever we were getting into, we were getting into it together. Why, even Bob Krassner and I spoke civilly to each other.

This was the real thing.

None of us had ever been up higher than the top of an SST's trajectory; none of us had ever been in real space. The eight of us were strongly aware of the bond of mingled fear and anticipation that linked us: apprentice spacemen—fledgling astronauts. It made me see everything in a new light. The sunshine that washed over us as we left the hotel and entered the cars for the airport, the air that blew in my face from the rolled-down window of the car on the drive... I felt and experienced it all as though it was the first time I had ever encountered it—and maybe the last, as well.

When our shuttle jet dropped down over the sprawling Cape, I stared at the sunwashed patterns of concrete on sand and felt my stomach knot and the hairs at the nape of my neck stiffen. The tall oblongs of the two Vertical Assembly Buildings cast clean dark shadows across the tiny moving dots of cars and service trucks that scurried like ants from mound to mound. The tall needle of the transport rocket stood sharply on its launch pad, still attached to its umbilical tower, the crawler-transporter that had brought it there creeping back toward its Assembly Building so slowly that to me it seemed to be standing still.

Bix pointed over my shoulder: "Our rocket!"

"Yeah," I said quietly. I did not want to talk. This was something personal, something between me and that vast launching complex below. I wanted to see everything, file it away in my memory where I could never lose it, and without distractions. Bix seemed to sense that. He said nothing more.

Then we'd passed over the area, and were in our landing pattern, the braking flaps on the wings of our plane dropping lower and lower until they were almost a second wing at right angles to the first, pointing at the ground, grabbing air, and slowing us so quickly that I felt the drag pulling me forward in my seat against the seat belt.

We dropped, almost straight down, it seemed, until suddenly there was concrete under us, the joints rushing past us in a smooth blur, and a moment later we were down with a squeal of tires, a light jolt, and were taxiing off the strip.

"We're here," somebody behind me said, and everyone seemed to let his breath out all at once. My fingers were a little numb and it took me two tries to get my belt unbuckled.

Bix gave me one of his dark smiles, and nodded. We shook hands, and then climbed to our feet.

Secret of the Marauder Satellite

Going out the door was like stepping into a blast furnace. I'd forgotten what Florida in the summertime could be like. I was wearing a light summer suit, and it seemed to be only seconds after I'd started down the ramp to the bright concrete that it was clinging smotheringly to me.

I sweat easily, and I could feel it standing all over my face by the time I'd hurriedly climbed into the waiting car. There were three cars waiting for us, and mine at least was air-conditioned. I said a few kind words to myself on the subject of air conditioning, and then took them back as Krassner pushed his way in next to Bix and me, somehow managing to take over half the back seat to himself.

"Sheesh, is it hot!" he said, flexing his arms and gouging Bix in the ribs with his elbow.

"Close the door, stupid!" I told him, "and keep your mouth shut, and it'll be a lot less hot in here."

Farnsworth, sitting between our driver and Gene Carr, twisted around in his seat and gave me a Piercing Look, but said nothing. It seemed likely he would be glad to see the end of me.

With the doors closed, it cooled down pretty fast. The windows were tinted, and they not only kept a lot of direct sun heat from getting in, they made it possible for me to see a little better. With a strong summer sun bouncing off all that white and unpainted concrete, you better believe it can get pretty dazzling.

I won't try to describe the next twenty minutes. We followed a mazelike series of roads, past all kinds of buildings, some looking like temporaries meant to be torn down ten years ago, some beautiful designs in poured concrete with green grass lawns and built-in sprinkler systems that cast a gauzy rainbow effect over them. Everywhere there were cars, cars of all types. Black government cars, olive-drab military cars, light blue NASA cars, cars from the different associated servicing companies with company decals on the doors; cars parked and cars moving, cars with single occupants, cars chauffeured by men in livery or uniforms, cars filled with shirt-sleeved, brown-tanned men; cars all with one thing in common: the windows were closed—all were air-conditioned. Somehow that struck me as the most profound observation I'd ever made at the Cape.

It's a busy place, and growing all the time. When the first Vertical Assembly Building was built for the Saturn moon rockets, back in the mid-sixties, the government was justifiably proud of it. It's fifty-two stories tall, and covers eight acres. It's so big that it has its own interior weather conditions, because if they didn't keep a very sophisticated air-conditioning system in operation, clouds might form up near the ceiling, and they might get rain.

But of course since then we've been using the Orion-type rockets, and by a peculiar coincidence, they just happen to be a little too big for the first Assembly Building, so we have Building #2. This one is sixty stories tall, and just right. I once asked one of my instructors what was to stop them from coming up with a bigger class of rocket, which would require its own, larger Assembly Building. He gave me a long lecture, which boiled down to: They won't. It seems that we're too sophisticated in our engine designs now to need bigger rockets, and in all likelihood, the future evolution of Earth-based rockets will be smaller, rather than bigger. If we need bigger ones, we'll assemble them in orbit.

At any rate, even without the need for a third building, there is still plenty of construction going on all the time at the Cape. And of course there's a lot of construction that has nothing to do with new launching facilities, like all the streets we crossed that were dug up on one side for newer, bigger, or better (or all three—take your pick) gas, water, or some such utility services.

A busy place, as I said.

We ended up in a medical reception center, where we were put through a fast final physical, and given our shots. These were antinausea shots, designed to save us from making messes when our inner ears told us down was up, or that we weighed the wrong amount. We'd already been fitted for our space suits, and had ten hours time in the simulators with them, so they were no real problem. We zipped into our knit, one-piece jump suits, climbed into our space suits, were tested out to make sure all the servomechanisms were functioning, and then waited.

The waiting was what nearly got me. I complained about it later, to a corpsman, and was razzed about it, but it bugged me; it really did. It seems as though government service—any branch—is mostly spent waiting. Red tape I'd heard about, been warned about. But this waiting! I'm used to fine-point efficiency. I was brought up on it. Throughout Space School we learned efficiency. It's part of survival. Space is the last—and biggest—frontier. You learn to do things well, or you don't have another chance. That's efficiency: Learning to do the most with the least effort. It's economy, but it's also pushing yourself to the maximum, doing *everything* you can do at this moment, *right now*. It's learning the fastest and easiest way to suit up, for instance. It's arranging in advance so that when you're finished with one job, the next is lined up and ready for you, but hasn't been waiting more than a moment. It's making things dovetail neatly together, rather than arranging things sloppily, and ending up with a mess. It appeals to me. It always has. I like to see the gears mesh cleanly, smoothly, with no grinding. I like to do things without wasted effort.

I like to be efficient.

But there is, I learned, a limit to efficiency. It has something to do with Parkinson's Law, which is something Bix told me about: "The more people you put on a job, the less work will get done."

The government is huge—its services embrace the whole country. It seems as though everything is getting too big these days for private industry—or that, left to private industry, needed things, things which wouldn't make a profit, just wouldn't get done. So the government steps in—*somebody* has to—and does it.

And that's where Parkinson comes in. There are too many people in civil service. Why, *I'm* in civil service, if it comes to that: NASA is a government agency, after all. And while an operation works efficiently on a local level (*if* there's a good administrator!), just try it on a national scale ...

Take us. We arrived on the Cape at 11:35. We were finished being put through the mill by 13:00. And liftoff was for 17:05.

It's true, they could've juggled things around to save waiting time, but it would've been at the expense of some other operation.

We would lift at 17:05, and that was that. We had a comparatively narrow "window"—six minutes—for which to shoot, and there would be no deviation there. But nobody wanted to be caught half finished with anything by then, either. So they allowed "slack time." They figured on traffic tie-ups between our hotel and the airport. They figured on something, maybe bad-weather conditions, forcing a premature landing. They figured, for all I know, on a volcano erupting between the landing field and the medical reception center. They figured on delays of every sort, delays we had no reason to expect, but which might just crop up *anyway*, and figured it out so that we'd still be ready to lift at 17:05.

Of course, everything had gone off without a hitch, so there we were, with four hours to kill. That's bureaucratic efficiency for you.

I don't know whether I need to explain that business about the launch "window" or not. Some of these things are so much a part of my training that I take them for granted—and then when I mention them in a casual conversation with a civvy, all I get is a blank stare.

It's this way: The Station is in a permanent orbit. It, like most of the satellites launched originally from Kennedy, is on an equatorial orbit—it follows the equator in its path around the Earth, rather than looping over the poles, as most of the small military observation satellites launched from the West Coast do. Now, to send a rocket up to meet the Station is a feat of very precise ballistics. Although a rocket is self-powered, and can change course, and do other relatively sophisticated things, it's really pretty much a big bullet, being fired at a moving target. It's like trying to bring down a duck with a rifle—or whatever it is hunters do on heavily overcast late-fall mornings—you follow that duck along with your gun, and you fire, not at the point where it is, but at where it will *be*, by the time your bullet gets up there.

Now, suppose you couldn't move your gun much; you couldn't follow the bird with it. Then, assuming the silly creature flies overhead at all, there will be only a fleeting moment when you can fire, and hit that bird. That moment is your "window." Fire at the beginning of the "window" and you'll hit the bird's head; a split second later, and you'll graze tail feathers.

The Station is, proportionately, a much tinier target, moving faster, and vastly farther away. But the "bullet"—in our case a Saturn "C" rocket—is maneuverable to some extent, and the whole shot is in the hands of a hair-triggered computer system. So there would be a six-minute period during which we could fire and make it into that sector of space—our actual "window"—where we would intersect the Station . . . and, on top of everything else, at compatible velocities.

Let me footnote that: It's all very well to shoot a bullet at a bird and make a hit, but we did not want to stretch the analogy that far; we did not want to shoot down, or wound, the Station. Instead, we had to cut things so fine that, having boosted ourselves into the same orbit, we would coast right into a landing bay at the Station. This means matched velocities. There are a lot of tricky parts to the problem; for instance, it requires a specific velocity to maintain any given orbit at a given distance from Earth's surface. A faster velocity means a higher orbit; a slower velocity will drop you closer to the surface. Clear? Now let's suppose you gained orbit—the same orbit as the

Station: the same "track" over the same parts of the world, at the same height—but on the opposite side of the world from the Station.

What do you do?

You can't try just to stop and hang there, waiting, till the Station comes up from behind. Try that, and Mother Gravity exerts her hold, and you plummet straight down like a meteorite.

And, on the other hand, you can't just speed up and overtake the Station, either. Because your increase in velocity is going to elevate your orbit. By the time you've overtaken the Station, you'll be hundreds of miles higher.

That will give you a rough idea of the problems the computers had to handle, and why, on any given day, there was only a brief moment when a successful shot could be made.

I've boiled it down, of course. There are sophisticated answers to the problems I mentioned—with the right equipment and knowledge, you *can* catch up with, or drop back to, a station on the opposite side of the world. And, sometimes, you are faced with solving problems like that yourself, as I was later to find out.

At about 16:00, they put us in a bus, and took us out to the launching pad.

This one being a passenger pad, there were permanent facilities, like a decent waiting room, with piped-in music, an underground shuttle to the tower elevator, and a certain civilian look which you won't find outside of consumer-oriented facilities. I half expected to see one of those machines where a quarter gets you flight insurance.

We were still milling around gawking at things when five newcomers entered, also suited up. We all had our helmets slung back on our shoulders, so I don't know why it took me as long as it did, but at first I did not recognize the Cramers.

Bix nudged me. "Look—it's your girl friend, and parent."

Mary waved at me and started over. Dr. Cramer remained with the other three men—Station staff members, I rightly guessed.

"Hi, Paul," Mary said. She was grinning hugely.

"Hi," I said, with less enthusiasm. I did not care to have Mary pegged by one and all as my "girl friend." We just happened to go on TV together; that's all.

"You're going up with us?"

"Sure—didn't I tell you?"

"Well, no."

"It must've been all that excitement about the park and everything. Sure. That's why we were in the same hotel as you. We had a different plane down, though. They never let Daddy go anywhere without a huge security guard." She winked. "He's supposed to be very valuable."

"But, I, ummm... I mean, uhh, why are you going up with us?" I managed to ask.

She flashed the happy-puppy smile at me again. "I managed to con Daddy into taking me. He's been wanting an assistant. You know—somebody who can do all his paperwork without messing it all up—and I managed to convince him that I'd make a better assistant than anyone else they're likely to give him. I mean, I've been reading over Daddy's shoulder since I was five." She stopped, breathless.

"Who's your friend?" she asked suddenly.

"Oh! Umm, this is Bix," I said. "Bix Beiderbecke."

Mary gave Bix a funny look, and then scowled at me. "You're putting me on."

"Huh?"

"I'm not stupid. I know who Bix Beiderbecke is—was, I mean."

"I'm a distant relative," Bix said.

"Wait a minute," I cut in. "Clue me in. What's this jazz all about?"

Mary smiled, then winked at Bix. That put me on my guard. "You mean you don't know?" she asked.

"I never heard the name before I met Bix," I said truthfully.

"Well, you put your finger on it, anyway."

"How's that?"

"'All this jazz,'" Bix said cryptically.

"My father has a big collection of his records," Mary said. "All on those funny old-fashioned ones that break."

"*Whose* records?" I shouted. Several heads turned inquiringly. I did my best to throttle my temper down. I don't like being kidded. Not like this, anyway. It's too much like being put deliberately on the outside. I've had enough of that, anyway.

Both of them seemed to realize the joke had run its course.

"Bix Beiderbecke," Mary said.

"My distant relative," Bix said.

"He was a jazz musician."

"You know—Dixieland, rinky-tinky-tink-tink."

"No, Chicago-style. He played a good cornet, and piano too."

"Well, he died young, anyway."

"He's the one they used for that book *Young Man with a Horn*," Mary said.

"But it wasn't exactly factual," Bix added.

"O.K., O.K.," I said. I held up my hands. "So in some fields I am ignorant. About music I know nothing, except that once when I was whistling in the shower somebody told me to shut up before I cracked all the mirrors."

They both laughed.

"*Attention, everyone. Please assemble at the loading doors.*" It was a PA announcement. I glanced at the chronometer on the inside of my wrist.

It was 16:35.

Chapter 4

I REMEMBER THE first time I watched a launching at the Cape. I was a first-year student at the Space School, and this was our first trip to see the Cape. I was pretty cool about it; after all, I'd seen plenty of launchings on TV, and we'd studied filmstrips which broke liftsoff down into their slow-motion components already.

But it was different when the two dozen of us stood in a hushed group in the local-control blockhouse, each of us straining for a glimpse through the heavy quartz windows, and alternating our attention to the closed-circuit color Sonies monitoring the launch.

Local-control had finished its technical countdown, and relinquished ground control to Houston, where the space-center computers were counting out the last second of the actual countdown.

Somebody once told me that the countdown is a gimmick thought up by the makers of an early German science fiction movie, to add suspense. But it's a vitally important procedure that is followed exactly with every launch.

Look at it this way: A countdown is not a man droning, "T minus blah seconds." A countdown is a final checkout of every functioning aspect of the rocket system. It's like starting a car. You follow a prescribed pattern. Key into ignition, ignition on, a check of instruments—gas O.K., battery isn't dead—and then the starter. That's simple, though, and nothing much happens if you goof the "countdown" in starting a car.

The countdown really started with the airplane. When you fly an airplane (and I know something about this; I've had several hours as a student in a small plane), you have to check out all sorts of things before you get off the ground—or else. A pilot has a list of items to be checked: Drain water from the gas tanks, check the oil level, test the controls, check the instruments—all the little things that add up to a plane being in proper shape for flying. The fellow who took up the plane I was training in after I did, by the way, got cocky. He didn't stick to the list, because he figured that if I had just used it, he was O.K. He checked the oil in a big hurry and didn't get the pressurized cap back on. He lost oil pressure, oil, and engine—in that order—at 3,000 feet, and his instructor made a soft landing in somebody's bean field. The plane flipped over only once, and nobody was hurt.

A rocket is a lot more sophisticated. Its engines are simpler, but its auxiliary equipment takes hours to check out. There are all the guidance systems to check out for proper response: the inboard computer system, the booster couplings—and, of course, the entire relay system between the Cape and Houston, and all the rest.

A modern countdown is simply a long list with every functioning servomechanism or system on it, with a checkout for each. And you have to time it all so that the rocket is ready for launching at the proper moment.

We've attained a pretty good state of the art by now; things usually come off nicely, without a glitch. But there's always the chance that some minor part will cause trouble and delay the whole shoot—so there's always tension in the air until the technical countdown is complete. Then the computers take over, and all that's left is to fire the rocket at the mathematically proper moment.

Now the technical men in the blockhouse were leaning

back, their job over. Everything was "All systems go" and locked onto automatic. For them, this was just another launch, and as good as finished. For us kids, the drama would be in the moment of ignition, and that's what we waited for.

Then it came!

A quarter of a mile away, the flat bright noontime vista was shattered by the frightening roar of the giant Saturn engines, and on the Sonies we could see the bright torch of the exhaust blackening out the center of the TV screens, while white clouds boiled up around the launch pad.

Thunder came up through the floor of the blockhouse, into the soles of my feet, and I was grabbed by a feeling of terrible awe—the overwhelming knowledge that I was a very junior member of the race that had conquered nature and the vastness of space and had built *that:* an unbelievably powerful engine of exploration, a probing needle that hovered for only moments over its pad and then arched up, high into the sky, climbing into the towering heavens— into the realm of the gods.

It seemed to me then a frighteningly audacious thing Man had done: a challenge to the Creator that could not be left unanswered, whether by reward or punishment, I did not know. For all of his history, Man had walked the surface of his planet, or sailed the surface of its oceans, learning to fly only a brief time ago, as history is reckoned, and then little higher than the birds.

Now Man was liberating himself of his natural dimension, daring a frontier more vast and terrible than any before it. I felt that, and it scared me. It also made me tremblingly proud, so proud to be a part of this vast quest that I felt the tears in my eyes and knew I was crying without embarrassment. I wasn't the only one.

The Cape has affected me like that ever since. It's been hard really to control my emotions; I feel as if I have been reduced to something elemental and very small—yet very important, in the scheme of things. These are thoughts and feelings I've kept mostly to myself, but I know that others have thought and felt them; Bix has, and so has Mary, and she says her father too.

The waiting room had been built in a concrete bunker—although the decorators had been at pains to disguise the fact—buried far below the actual launching pad on which our rocket sat. There were tunnels and elevators leading to the control blockhouse, and to the outside, but only one short tunnel to the elevator that was waiting for us now. The thirteen of us ordered ourselves into lines, the men in the lead, each of us suited up and carrying only what personal gear we could fit into the suit kit provided for such items as toothbrushes and the like. There was no one there to say good-by; our farewells had already been said. One by one we walked down the short tunnel, past the heavy bulkhead doors that would seal the tunnel off from any blow-by blast, and into the simple cagelike elevator.

There was little talking. "This is it, huh?" I nodded to Bix, and he winked back. This was it. The climaxes were past.

The cage door to the elevator slid automatically shut. We were standing on a platform, surrounded by a wire-link fence higher than our heads. Except for the boxlike girder structure that formed the skeleton of the elevator, the top was open. I could see a long shaft with light at the top, cables snaking up along the sides. They tightened and began to sway, back and forth. We were going up.

The shaft ended at the surface of the pad, and for a moment our eyes were level with the base of our rocket, but the elevator was still climbing, half its journey still to be done.

Now we were swinging up past an open latticework of girders, the umbilical tower that would hold and support the rocket almost until ignition, and the elevator cables were singing with vibration.

Now we felt the heat of the open, the sun slanting down at us through the tower, shadows flickering over us. I was grateful for the way space suits had been modified and lightened; early astronauts had to carry portable air conditioners during this part of their journey to keep from roasting in their suits. But it still seemed to me foolish that we were required to suit up for the trip; the Russians discarded the practice long ago. Of course, their ships have airlocks too. On the other hand, Dr. Cramer pointed out to me later a point I'd overlooked.

"Paul, you have to have a suit once you're up here—everyone does. It's needed for your work, and it's an absolutely necessary safety precaution. How do you suppose your suit would've gotten up here, if you hadn't carried it on your back?" Too true.

The trip up that tower seemed as slow as the part in the shaft had been fast. It reminded me of a roller-coaster ride I'd once taken—the first part, while the cars are clanking up the first incline. As we'd gotten higher and higher, the cars had seemed to go slower and slower, heightening the suspense.

Soon we were abreast the second stage, and the panorama of the launch complex and the Cape was spread out below us. The sky overhead was very blue.

Then with a slight shudder, the elevator came to a stop. The gate slid open. Ahead of us was the entrance to the capsule.

We use the Saturn C for commuting to the Station rather than the smaller rockets we'd originally used for orbiting trips, because of the payload—the number of passengers—we carry each trip. The C capsule can accommodate up to fourteen passengers, although it does the job rather the same way sardine packers do.

We entered through the port in the nose. Inside there was a series of ladder rungs leading down toward what was now the bottom, and would soon be the back, of the capsule. Down there were four acceleration couches. The first four men in climbed down and into their seats. They then reached forward and released the next four couches, which had been folded against the side. These pivoted out over the bottom row, hiding the first four men from sight, and locked into place almost directly over them. Mary, Bix, and I settled into these; to my vast annoyance, Bob Krassner plunked himself down next to me.

We each reached up and triggered the releases on the couches over us, and in the next moment I was fighting off a severe attack of claustrophobia.

Although I'd been in the simulators enough times to know how it felt to lie flat on your back with your knees brought up into a semicrouch, the contours of another acceleration couch only inches in front of your nose, no room really to shift about or even to cross your legs—this wasn't the same. For one thing, it smelled different. Don't ask me how, but it smelled *real*, not like a mock-up of fiber glass and cardboard. It was dark in there, and I felt pinned, trapped in a box—or (this from an old movie on the late, late show) in a coffin. But what I really think did it was feeling Krassner lying there right next to me, his elbow and shoulder nudging me, making me feel cramped and making me want to edge over, away from him— which was impossible, since that would be crowding Bix.

I can tell you, I felt pretty uncomfortable.

There were grunts from the guys overhead climbing into their couches, then the clicks as they released the top two couches. I wish I could've been in either one of the outside couches on the third row, or one of the two on the top row—then, at least, I'd have had a little breathing space.

A metallic voice from a speaker asked, *"Everyone settled? Roll call."*

We each spoke our name in turn. I was surprised; Dr. Cramer and his three associates sounded off just as we cadets did. Mary's voice broke when it was her turn, and I heard Bix whisper something to her afterward. I don't know what it was, but it was probably the right thing; she giggled.

"O.K.," the speaker said after a pause. *"It is now T minus 920 seconds, and counting."*

I was glad of that. About fifteen minutes left—the waiting was nearly at an end. The port was being dogged, and soon, I knew, the tower would be moving away from us.

We had no pilot; it was unnecessary. We were in a passenger capsule—a third stage that would be guided directly by Houston until docking time, when the Station would take us over. We were just so many fish in a can, under shipment. There would be an equal number of returnees to take our places on the capsule's return as well, all bundled the same way into this ultimate elevator. Everything was fully automated. Those daring space pilots of the old TV serials had never had a chance....

The speaker droned the final seconds into a flat silence that gripped us all. Then, somewhere far below us, there began a distant roaring.

The roar ascended the scale until it was a vibration we felt, rather than heard—and soon that was gone too.

My couch had pushed up around me, and I found myself sinking back into it with the thrust of the acceleration, and all the time staring at the couch so close overhead. *I hope it holds,* I was saying over and over to myself. *I just hope it holds.* I dug the gloved fingers of my hands into the foam-covered handrests and if they'd been oranges, I'd have gotten all the juice out.

Of course the seat held; it was designed to.

I don't know how long I was lying there grabbing on for dear life, but after a while it occurred to me that the sounds had disappeared, there was less thrust holding me down, and that I wasn't going to get squeezed flat by the guy in the couch overhead.

There was a solid *ka-thunk,* and then another, weaker thrust. The third stage booster had blown free, and we were using the second stage now. Soon we would be floating, in free fall, as we coasted out toward our rendezvous with the Station.

"*A good launch,*" came the words from the speaker.

"Everything on the nose. You're in the groove; you'll be docking in seventy-five minutes."

Just then the acceleration stopped. There was another, closer jar, and I knew we'd separated from the second stage.

We were coasting now. We were in free fall.

Not that we were likely to float anywhere. Each of us was strapped down, and even if we hadn't been, we couldn't have gotten far.

The announcement from Houston Control broke the tension, and everyone started talking. Bob Krassner strained his face over toward me in the gloom and said in a whiny voice, "Why can't they put windows back in this part of the capsule? You know, so we could see out?"

It bothered me too, but I wasn't going to let him see that. "Unlax," I said, "you'll get plenty of space in the next six months."

"Yeah, I know, but that's not the same. I mean, I wanted to watch liftoff—I wanted to look out and see the old Mother Earth drop away, the way they do it on TV. I—urps," he said. He brought his hand up over his mouth. "I—I feel kinda funny," he said weakly.

"You're not going to get sick, are you?" I asked. I was pretty concerned. I mean, I was right next to him, after all, and he was facing me. "You had your shots, didn't you?"

He nodded, but didn't open his mouth again.

"You'll be all right," I said hopefully.

He surprised me. He had the grace to turn his face toward the wall. Nevertheless, I hoped he wouldn't be sick. In free fall, stuff just floats around, moving with the air currents. It would be very messy.

Bix had been talking with Mary about something, but now he was lying back with his eyes closed.

"What's the matter? Are you sick too?"

He opened one eye for a moment, and then closed it again. "Nope. Just taking a nap. Best time for it; weightless sleep is the best you can get, and we don't know what time it'll be at the Station when we get there."

"A good idea, young man," came Dr. Cramer's voice floating up from the bottom layer. "There's very little else you *can* do, you know."

I stared at Bix in disgust. He'd finked out, and was leaving me for Krassner.

Speaking of whom...

"Hey, Williams—?"

"Shut up, Krassner. I'm trying to sleep," I said.

I amazed myself. I actually did fall asleep. I'd been afraid the first time I'd thought of life on the Station and sleeping in free fall—I didn't know much about the Station then—that I'd have nightmares, the kind where you fall. Floating, after all, is really the same as falling, from your body's point of view; that's what free fall means. I hadn't yet had a chance to try moving much in free fall, but I knew that if I hadn't had those shots, my stomach would've flipped over, and I'd have grabbed the nearest solid-looking object.

But maybe they'd slipped tranquilizers in along with the other shots, or maybe the antinausea shots were all it took; floating was just sort of dreamy... when my eyes closed it was hard to remember I had a body, and pretty soon I didn't...

I woke up to feel something tugging at me. It felt hours later, and I started to jerk up in panic. What had happened? Had I overslept? Had they overlooked me? What—?

It was one of the little maneuvering rockets, jockeying us around, lining us up for docking. I'd slept only a little over an hour. It felt like a full night.

That's what weightless sleep does for you. Bix explained it to me later: It allows a deeper sleep, and gives your body a more complete rest. They've experimented with special sleep chambers, down on Earth, which simulate floating and allow you to compress a night's sleep into a few hours, but nothing beats the real thing.

I wondered why the sleeping quarters on the Station

weren't weightless, and Bix explained to me, "Just ignoring the matter of physical space—I mean, how are you going to get everybody sleeping on the axis? Just ignoring that, there's the psychological factor. This is why those sleep experiments on Earth never added up to much. You see, you sleep for two reasons: for body rest, and for psychological reasons—to dream. I'm very much interested in that; it seems that you have to dream a certain percentage of time in order to stay mentally healthy. Now, according to Jungian theory—" At that point I'd cut him off.

I looked to my left, and saw that Bix was also awake.

"We'll be docking soon," he said. "How do you feel, huh?"

"Oh, great," came a voice from the other side of me. "Just great. First we don't get to see liftoff—now we miss seeing the Station. Boy!"

"Hey, Krassner!" came a voice from above. "Why don't you quit your bellyaching, huh?"

"That's all right for you—you're up there where you can see it all!"

And that's how we arrived at the Station—not with a bang, but a whine.

Chapter 5

SOME OF THE old-timers on the Station call it the Tin Can, and there's a good reason for that. Viewed from any distance, it does look like a tin can.

It started out a whole lot differently. It was the direct heir of the orbiting laboratory the Air Force put up in the early seventies. There was a lot of beefing about a manned military satellite, however, so NASA took the lab over, and began building additions.

The first lab was simply a short pipelike section that would barely hold two men in comfort. But it also held a lot of scientific gear.

NASA began orbiting new lengths that neatly fitted on the ends, extending the length and capacity of the Station. Then when they had a good-sized pipe, they began constructing a wheel around it, spokes radiating out from the central pipe to the rim. The original lab became the axis of the new Station, like a wheel mounted on an axle.

There was a very sound reason for building the wheel instead of just continuing to lengthen the central pipe, and it had nothing to do with the complaints of the early Station personnel about having to squirm the length of the pipe every time they wanted a different tool or instrument. What it boiled down to was the need for weight: some of the work simply could not be done under weightless conditions.

We haven't figured out how to make artificial gravity or antigravity yet—although that's bound to be the next step in space travel—but we can simulate gravity in an age-old way: centrifugal force.

Swing a ball on a string around your head, and it will exert a force *away* from your hand. This force is equal no matter whether the ball is above or below your hand, no matter from which direction gravity is pulling. Or—fill a pail half full of water, and start turning your body around, swinging the pail in a circle, and pretty soon the pail is on its side—but the water is still glued to its bottom.

So they built a wheel around the old lab, and they rotated the wheel on the axis of the old lab, and out on the wheel itself they had a very respectable sort of pseudo-gravity: the outside of the wheel was "down" and the axis was "up." As you climbed a spoke toward the center axis, the effects of the spin became less—"gravity" was lighter—until once you were back at the center of things, in the old lab, you were again weightless, and could float in the center while the walls revolved around you.

The military stepped in again—the cold war seemed to be getting a little hotter about then—and demanded a share of "their" Station. NASA graciously let them build a second wheel, so that the Station now looked like two wheels at each end of an axle. The military boys have always kept their quarters very hush-hush, but it is known that they imported a number of missiles with nuclear warheads, and a lot of ballistic computers.

Since space within the Station is always a bit cramped, despite the vast expansion over its original size, it was decided to enclose the two wheels in a cylinder, and close off the ends between the spokes. This turned the Station into the shape it is now: a vast spinning barrel, with two nubby fingers pointing out of each end to mark the original axis.

Naturally, all this building took an awful lot of material—most of it plain sheet metal. Although this sheet metal would cost very little on Earth, F.O.B., Gary, Indiana, it cost quite a lot more to boost it into orbit. The Station has been under construction for almost fifteen years, now, and is far from finished.

Well, anyway, that's how the Station evolved. Physically, it measures two thousand feet long, and three hundred sixty feet in diameter. In addition to the main "can," there are those two "fingers" pointing out each end that I told you about. One of them is an observatory, the other the docking facilities. Both are coupled to the Station in such a way that they do not turn with the Station's rotation; gyroscopes hold them in a position fixed relative to Earth.

The Station doesn't sound very big the way I've described it—and it doesn't even look that big when you're close by in space. But it is big—it is the biggest thing Man has ever put into space. It's as big in volume as a large office building—and the interior space is a whole lot more efficiently arranged.

A good deal of the interior isn't finished off yet, of course. That's what we're still building. The outer shell is in place, and under pressure; we have air throughout. But many of the levels haven't been put in yet, and venturing into the uncompleted parts is like wandering into a vast and empty warehouse.

There are a lot of unusual problems in building and maintaining a station that spins as this does. The most important is that of balance. This not only means that we have to build equally all around the perimeter, putting equal amounts of mass opposite each other, but that we must be careful about the actual movement of the Station personnel. If all the people moved into one area, it would seriously throw the whole Station out of kilter. Think of it like the wheels on your family car; they have to be balanced, or the tires wear unevenly, a wobbling vibration sets up at certain speeds, and you get a very rough ride.

Well, if the Station got seriously out of balance, it would wobble too. And that wobble, unless caught very quickly, would feed itself, build, and increase—not only throwing us and every movable item all over the place, but throwing the Station itself out of its stable orbit.

So we have this computer system that does nothing but keep track of the movements of everyone in the Station. And when minor imbalances occur, it shifts ballast. And the ballast? I'm glad you asked me that question. The ballast is our water. Rather than keeping the water in central tanks, it has been distributed through a network of valves and pipes all over the rim of the Station.

—Hmm. Bix, who is reading this over my shoulder, points out that I am exaggerating the dangers of an imbalance and the real chances for setting up a wobble. He's right. We humans aboard the Station don't represent a very sizable percentage of the total mass. The inertial effects of the mass of the structure itself are rather like that of a flywheel, evening out minor imbalances. Nonetheless, the situation bothered enough people that we've got the ballasting system we do, and of course it has to compensate for shifts in equipment and things like that, as well. And I've heard NASA crewmembers quietly cursing the military boys, who apparently spend most of their time moving their missiles around.

Anyway, I think my point is still a good one. There's a lot more to keeping this Station spinning than meets the eye.

Our C capsule slid smoothly into the docking collar. It was so smooth that I hardly felt a jar.

"Hey—what's going on up there?" Krassner demanded. "Tell us what you can see."

"Can't see anything now," Carr's voice answered. "We slid in past the collar, and everything's dark.—Wait a minute!

"Yeah, the lights just came on. We're sticking into a big chamber—a big, circular chamber. There's a big round port directly facing us, and . . . yeah, it's starting to open."

Carr paused, and Krassner asked, "Yeah, yeah—now what?" Sometimes I had to appreciate the guy. I was as curious as he was.

"Some guys are coming through—they're floating, pushing themselves off the walls. One of them is right over the viewport—"

We could all hear the metallic sounds as the hatch was undogged.

Then a new voice spoke.

"Hello, there. You're docked; ease on out."

I heard the top two guys—one of them was Carr, I guess—unsnapping their seat belts.

"Easy, now. Keep a hold on something. There's a line fastened outside for you to follow, and somebody to help you. Just stick to your disembarking routine.... Right... easy there ... "

Then they were climbing out of the seats over us, and a few moments later the seats flew up against the walls, and I could see.

A crewmember who looked maybe twenty-three, but at the same time infinitely older and more experienced than I felt, was grinning at us. He was wearing a blue jump suit—they look almost like long johns, but that's what everybody wears on the Station—and he leaned out over us, hanging almost—from my point of view—upside down, his feet hooked into the laddered handholds.

"Well, there: a young lady! How do you do, Miss? Right this way ... that's right."

Mary unbuckled and reached tentatively up for his hand. He took it, and pulled her smoothly up, in an almost liquid motion.

"Remember," he said, "you'll keep going in whatever direction you're aimed at, without losing speed. Take it slow and easy at first; it saves a lot on sprained wrists and broken arms. You next, fella." Mary had wriggled her way through the port and her slender legs were just disappearing from sight.

Bix was next and he executed the whole maneuver smoothly and easily, slipping through the port like an eel.

The man had a firm grip, and I found myself being catapulted in slow motion, up out of my couch toward the nose of the capsule and the port.

And then I was falling.

Suddenly the nose and the port were no longer *up*. They were *down*, and I was falling straight down!

I panicked for a moment, and windmilled my arms and legs, trying to get a grip on the air, grab a handhold—anything!—anything to slow me down, check my fall.

What I did was to spin my body around, so that my feet were the first to touch the rim of the port.

I caught hold of myself then, and remembered my training. *The most important thing was not to push out with my legs to check my "fall."* I remembered the filmed footage an instructor had shown us of a man deliberately faking a panic reaction in free fall. Every time he grabbed for something, he went ricocheting off on a new course, sometimes at a fairly good speed. *"Remember,"* my instructor had said, *"you may be weightless, but you'll have as much mass and inertia as ever. You can still smash yourself up, plowing into a wall, unchecked, even when you're as light as a feather."*

I let my knees collapse, as my legs absorbed the gentle impact, and I doubled over until my hands had a good grip on the port rim. Then, being careful to keep a good handhold, I pulled myself through.

The crewman was looking up at me when I glanced back over my shoulder, and the expression on his face was close to a sneer. "Just can't resist showing off, eh?"

I choked back the reply I was going to make. If he wanted to take my moment of panic for a show-off maneuver, who was I to disillusion him? Besides, I was holding things up as it was.

While another crewman watched, I started docilely hand over hand down the knotted rope to the open port up ahead.

Behind me I heard a sudden shrill squeal of pain. Krassner had done it again.

Once through the port, I found myself in a large air lock, a chamber bigger than the docking chamber. As I pulled myself through, still following the rope with its knots spaced easily every foot, I tried to see as much as I could without throwing off the body rhythm that was moving me so smoothly along. I had glimpses of spidery skeletal frameworks, with spheres and cylinders fastened to them, the latter looking like naked rocket engines. Then I was through the open port on the opposite wall.

Ahead of me was a long straight tube, with people clinging to its sides. As I hung, momentarily, before them, they spun around me in a counterclockwise motion.

Another man in blue reached out and grabbed me, swinging me around and toward the wall.

The next moment I was crouched against the wall, my arms through handholds, and a feather-light gravity gently urging me to stay where I was.

I looked up, over my shoulder, and saw, only ten feet away, Ralph Ward, looking down, over his shoulder at me. We were clinging to the wall of the tube directly opposite each other.

But we weren't spinning anymore.

Or rather I could no longer feel the tube spinning. Everything seemed stationary, except for the port at the end of the tube: the body just emerging from it was being twisted about, counterclockwise.

"Yeesh!" he said. "Oh, my aching stomach!" It was Krassner, of course. The crewmen laughed good-naturedly. "Come on in, Cadet," said the one who'd grabbed me. "Get your toes wet."

Once we were all together, we were led to a shaft, and the crewman in charge of us pointed down the shaft, saying, "Think of that as an elevator shaft. You could fall down that shaft and die."

I was still disoriented. I hadn't quite established

"down" yet, but at the same time, I was no longer quite weightless. This shaft, painted a light yellow like the tube we were in, looked like just another corridor, its only real difference being that it was a square shaft instead of tubular.

"This is a shaft that leads to the rim," the crewman said. "If you fell down that shaft, you'd pick up quite a lot of speed before you hit the bottom—and gravity is about Earth-normal down there. That's a 180-foot shaft—that's around eighteen or twenty stories. Think of it that way."

"Uhh, sir?" It was Mark Atwood.

"Yes?"

"Why would you fall? I mean, maybe it's one-G down there, but it sure isn't up here."

"No, it isn't. But let's say you went scooting down that shaft, thinking it was a horizontal corridor, instead. Well, the Station is spinning. And this shaft is one of the spokes the Station is spinning on. It's moving, you know, and moving around the axis of the area we're in now. What might start out as a weightless jump would pretty soon fetch you up against the west wall. And then, unless you had a fast handhold, you'd be rolling and sliding right down to the bottom."

"Well, sir, it looks to me as though the handholds are all on the side you'd come up against, so what's the problem?"

"Very observant. Not only that, the exit at each level is on the same wall of the shaft, for the same reason. But you're forgetting something. Up here you're going to have to learn a whole new set of reflexes, and not just one set, either. You're going to have to learn to handle yourself in null-g—complete weightlessness—and in every variation up to full g, down at S Level. Every level you'll be on will have a slightly different weight. A simple step on Level S would carry you across a good-sized room on Level G—got it? You're going to have to watch yourselves closely.

"For your convenience—and ours—we've color-coded the different areas. You! What color is the area we're in now?" His finger was jabbing at me.

"Umm, yellow, sir."

"Very good. What do you suppose that means?"

"Not having seen any other areas, I'd have to guess, sir. I'd guess yellow is for near-weightless areas and, maybe,"—I glanced down the shaft again; yes, it was the same shade—"maybe dangerous areas."

He smiled. "You score 100 percent, Cadet. That's what it is: yellow means caution—take no chances.

"As for the rest of the areas, red means real danger: Never enter a red area unless authorized. It may mean an area under construction, or an area where there's a likely pressure drop, or something else. For you cadets, red means 'stay out.' Got that?

"The rest of the levels are divided off into thirds. Levels B through G are tan; H through M are blue; N through S are green. Green means you can expect to be fairly safe with Earth-type reflexes. Since the largest part of the Station is in the green areas, that's where you'll be bunked, eat, and spend most of your time. But periodically you'll be sent up into the other areas, and you'll undergo training for those levels. O.K.? You got me? Let's go."

Using his hands, he flipped his body up and around, in an impossible handstand, swinging his legs over into the shaft, and catching his feet on the rungs of the ladder. Then, with fluid movements, he began to swarm down the ladder for the levels below.

For a moment we all hesitated; no one wanted to be first.

"O.K., Cadets! Let's snap to!" came the order from another crewman behind us.

For a moment I resented him; I resented them all. Accustomed as they were to living and working up here on the Station, unencumbered with space suits as we were, they found it very easy to set examples they knew we'd find hard to follow.

But I wasn't going to let them get my goat. "Unlax," I told myself. And then I half bounced, half crawled to the lip of the shaft.

It looked so easy, I thought. I could just crawl around the corner and in.

"Watch it, Cadet!" came the irritated shout behind me. It was the crewman who'd unloaded us from the capsule. "Get your head outta there! You want to break your neck?"

I swung around, and fished with my feet for the ladder rungs. Someone was snickering at me. I started a cautious descent.

It sure wasn't the way I'd expected it to be.

Chapter 6

THE NEXT COUPLE of hours were not particularly interesting. We were just a new crew of fledgling cadets as far as the crew was concerned. As soon as they'd hustled us through, they had the departure of the previous group of cadets, now seasoned by six months on the Station, to see to.

As for us, we were put through a brief indoctrination and taken out toward the living-quarters area of the Station to settle in. Dr. Cramer, his associates, and Mary all split off from us before the indoctrination, and I wasn't to see any of them again for some time.

We'd been assembled in a large room—well, large for the Station, anyway. The Station is engineered as a cross between a submarine and a house trailer: everything is very compact and efficient; there's no wasted space. Commander Davidson rose and addressed us. It was mostly a standard welcoming bit, but I was fascinated to see the commander in the flesh.

Commander Davidson looks about as much unlike a spaceman as you can imagine. And yet he was the man who made the Station what it is today, and will probably make our Lunar colonies working propositions someday.

He's short, and at first he looks fat. But that's really his beard. He wears a full beard, and his eyes twinkle. Bix says that exposure to direct sunlight naturally develops a squint in a man's eyes, and that the friendly paternal image the commander projects is just good psychology. I think he's a man who laughs a lot, and I like that. I don't care what his reasons are.

He is stout, though, and that, along with his shortness, and the full, rounded beard, gives him a sort of jolly look. He speaks very much like an old-fashioned gentleman. Of course, his speech, where he welcomed us to the Station and to space service, must be one he's delivered plenty of times before—every six months, now that I think of it—but he managed to make it sound personal and real, as if we were the first. But what I'm really thinking of, when I think about him, is my later contact with him, and his curiously gentle voice, polite, quiet, and friendly—yet firm and commanding. It's easy to understand how he got and held his job. I can't think of anyone up here who dislikes him. And yet, no one puts anything over on him.

After the brief indoctrination talk, we were taken to our quarters. These were on Level N, the topmost of the green levels.

"Can you feel any difference in the gravity?" I asked Bix. We were settling into our room—or rather, our cubicle. It had a bunk bed on one wall that was exactly as long as the wall. Under the bottom bed was a built-in set of drawers, in which we'd keep our possessions. At the moment, this didn't consist of much.

The rest of the room was bare; the only features marring the three walls were the outside door and the door to the closet—if you can call something a foot deep that—where we hung our space suits.

"Pseudogravity," Bix corrected me. "You want the top bunk or the bottom?

"Well, not really," Bix went on to answer my question, "but I've been so keyed up that I don't think I'm capable of fine discriminations."

I tried out both bunks. The bottom one had the top one

just over it, which made me feel claustrophobic. The top one was the same distance from the ceiling, and no improvement. "You're taller; you take the top," I said. "We can switch around later if we want to.

"Yeah, I know what you mean," I continued. "But I've been trying to catalog my reactions. You know, so I can start developing those different reflexes that fellow mentioned."

"Why?"

"What do you mean, 'why'?"

"Reflexes are an unconscious process. You'll develop them by experience."

I sprawled on the lower bunk, stripped now to my jump suit. "Maybe. But you can speed the process up if you try. I intend to try."

"It's important?" asked Bix.

"Yeah."

The silence dragged. I knew he wanted to ask why, and I felt like making him ask. If he wanted to practice being an analyst, he'd have to work at it.

"O.K.," he said, as if in answer to my thoughts. "Why?"

"Because this is more than a job—more than a training period for me," I said quietly. Deliberately, I tried to unlax, ease the tenseness in my muscles. "This is *space*. This is my career. This is where I make good. Or..."

"Or...?"

"Or I don't." I slammed my fist into the foam mattress. "So what's it to you? I want to try—I want to succeed. This is a big deal?"

"Is it?"

"O.K.—enough. Cool it, Dr. Beiderbecke. My hour is over."

"What happens if you don't make it?" Bix asked, his voice unperturbed, as though I'd said nothing.

"It's not going to happen," I said.

"I've read your records, you know," Bix said. "Your parents are alive and healthy. How come you never had any visits from them during the time you were at school? How come you never went home?"

"*Shut up!*" I said. I squeezed my eyes so tightly shut that tears squeezed out. "Quit your prying and leave me alone, willya? Just leave me alone."

"Sure, Paul," he said quietly, from somewhere over my head.

There are a lot of peculiarities in a station that is built like a barrel and that has a period of rotation of once every fifteen seconds. Although the pseudogravity of centrifugal force makes *out* appear *down*, there's also the angular velocity of that revolution every fifteen seconds. That's a fairly fast spin, and although *down* was the floor under my feet, there was a thrust from the direction of spin that had its own side effects. It made one direction uphill and the other downhill.

That doesn't sound just right; let me explain.

The A Level is the core of the barrel: the axis. The S Level is the one closest to the outer skin of the barrel. Normally, you think of one level being directly under the next, in flat planes. But here each level is wrapped around the core, in concentric circles. This means that you can follow a corridor on one level all the way around the Station and arrive back at where you started.

Very quickly we got used to using geographical terms in thinking of directions. The docking port was the north pole; the observatory at the opposite end of the Station the south pole. Those ends of the Station became the north and south. If you headed around the Station in the direction of the spin, you were heading east; against the spin was west.

Just standing where two corridors—an east-west and a north-south—crossed was a strange experience at first. The north-south corridors were long and straight, and you could see from one end to the other. But when you turned to look east or west, that corridor curved up, away from you in both directions.

Now, here's the hardest part to get used to: The corridor curved up exactly to the same degree to the east as it did to the west—and being the same corridor all the way around the Station, both ends met overhead, directly opposite—and the optical illusion was that if you went either way, you'd be walking uphill.

Of course, you're thinking, if you haven't already heard about this, *neither one* actually felt like uphill when you walked it—due to centrifugal force distributing its pseudogravity equally at all points, it should be like walking a flat floor.

Wrong. If you walk west, it's "uphill"; east is "downhill." That's what I started out to explain.

The reason is that angular velocity I mentioned. That's due to the amount of spin involved. When you are walking west, you are walking *against* the spin, against the angular velocity. It's not a lot, but it's there. It's the same thing that would push you against the side of one of those yellow shafts we were warned about. You can feel it when you're walking a north-south corridor, too, inching you over against one wall.

I once had a chance to ask Dr. Cramer about it—why didn't they angle the corridors a little, to compensate? Like banking a road on a turn?

He very kindly explained to me the engineering problems that would cause, the additional construction problems, the difficulties in lining up room entrances and corridors, and all the rest. When he was finished, my ears were burning, and I resolved to think things through all the way for myself the next time.

So life on the Station had its peculiarities, as I've said. It took a lot of getting used to. It meant training my eyes to see things as they were, rather than the way they *should* be, down on Mother Earth. It meant learning to lean a little to the east, when on a north-south route—and when going around to the other side of whatever level I was on, taking the easy way, "downhill," to the east. It meant developing a whole new set of senses which discriminated very subtle changes in the pseudogravity.

I had a chance to put my training to a test, too.

It was our second week, and we were still in General Instruction while we were getting our "space legs," as they put it. I'd made the mistake of asking our instructor, Charlie Wilimczyk, how much longer we were going to dawdle around before pulling down work assignments.

"You know, Williams," he said; "there's one like you in every bunch—the wise-guy know-it-all."

"I—"

"I heard about your little escapade leaving the capsule. I know your type: the tried and true spaceman, who just can't wait to show his stuff."

"Sir, I—"

"I'm speaking, Williams. What were you doing?"

"Interrupting, sir. You've—"

"That's right, Williams. Don't interrupt. Now, as I was saying...

"There's always one of you wise guys in every bunch: The born spaceman who can't wait to get out there and conquer space for Mother and Old Glory. Eh? You never can see why we want to train you properly first. Always impatient.

"Well, we have a little test for guys who ask your question."

"What is it, sir?"

"You'll find out soon enough. It's very simple. You'll report to me at the end of this class. Which will be, ummm, in fourteen minutes. In the meantime, you'll pay attention to our topic."

The topic was Welding in Different Air Densities. It was dull, and it was all stuff we'd gone over before. I could see that, and so could everybody else in the class. Just who did Wilimczyk think he was conning?

"This is the officers' elevator, Williams," Wilimczyk said. "It is off limits to cadets and normal crewmen, except at times like this. As you can see"—he waved his hand through the door—"it is quite small. It will normally accommodate only four people. Step in."

The interior was painted a cheerful canary.

"I—I thought yellow was reserved for warning areas."

"It is. This is a warning to you not to be caught in here unauthorized." There was an alphabetical bank of buttons by the door. Wilimczyk pushed one, and the door closed. He shifted his body until it hid the buttons.

"It's a very simple test, Williams. You will face the wall, away from the door. I will send the car to different levels. You will tell me which level we are on, or your best guess." His voice grew heavy on the last part, and I knew he expected me to guess wildly.

Would I? I wasn't sure. I'd done a lot of exploring on my free time, climbing up and down the levels, going all the way up to the lowest of the tan levels—a climb of some thirteen stories from the bottom, S, level. I'd tried to teach myself the differences in each level. But this wouldn't be the same, I knew. I'd never used an elevator before. I'd always gone from one level to the next, a level at a time, knowing where I was. This would be different.

A weight pressed against my knees, and we were rising. I wondered how fast the elevator was going. If the acceleration was any guide, fairly fast. I tried to count off the seconds, and imagine how many levels we would have passed in that time.

The car stopped, and behind me I heard the door swish open.

"May I, umm, bend my knees a little?" I asked. "To test it, I mean?"

I knew while I was asking the question that we'd come up a fair ways this time. The stop had lifted me on my feet more than it would've in a gravity close to that of the lowest levels.

"Sure; go ahead."

I lifted myself on my toes, then let myself down on my knees a little, trying to get the feel of the gravity. It felt close to a half-g. It felt like the middle of the blue levels.

"Uhh, Level J?" I guessed.

He said nothing, but the door closed. The car started down. He wasn't going to tell me how close I was. If there was an error in my figuring, it might increase with each stop, especially if I was trying to guess by the intervals between stops. I decided the elevator did not have variable speed controls. That would've been Too Much.

We stopped again. I flexed my legs again. "Around Level Q," I said.

"Around?"

"O.K.—Level Q!"

The doors closed again. We went up.

We went up. We went down. We went down again. We went up.

I judged we never went higher than Level F or G. I called it F. It felt a little lighter than G had, when I'd climbed up to it. We made twenty stops. Many were to the same levels, I was convinced. It was part of the plan to confuse me. If I'd been trying to cheat in any way, I'd have been confused. But I wasn't. It worked the other way around. I stopped paying attention to how long it took between levels. I waited until the doors opened, then took a step backward or forward, or just did a kneebend, and made my decision. And I became surer, less confused. The more data, the more certain I became.

Finally, we stopped again, and I said, "Level R." That was the level the instruction rooms were on.

"O.K.," Wilimczyk's voice held a different note. "That's it. All out."

It was Level R, of course.

They took me down to see Commander Davidson on Level S, three hours later.

He stared at a magic slate that was sitting before him on his desk. The desk was a metal top that folded down from the wall. His office was little bigger than my bunk room.

"H'mmm...Cadet Williams, yes?" He rose and shook my hand. "I'm very pleased to meet you, Williams. Yes, very pleased. It's not often we get a cadet of your caliber. Sit down."

There was one other seat in the tiny office; it too folded out from the wall. I perched myself on it and waited. Wilimczyk had put the slate on his desk. It would have my score on it. I couldn't read it from where I sat; the black lines on gray were lost in the reflection of the desk lamp on the acetate overlay sheet.

"Nineteen out of twenty," the commander said quietly. "You were wrong about the second one."

"It was actually Level P," I said. I'd become certain of it later.

"It was."

He looked up at me, and stared closely. I returned his stare. It didn't tell me much. I can't read expressions hidden by beards.

"You have an abnormally sensitive body," he said finally. "How are you on spatial relationships? Judging relative speeds, collision course, and near misses, that sort of thing."

"Very good, sir," I said. "I was a good automobile driver, and I took small-plane training on my own."

"You grasp three-dimensional movements, then." It was not quite a question.

"Yes, sir. I've played three-dimensional ticktack-toe, and 3-D chess—although I'm not a big chess buff."

"Too impatient, I bet."

"Yes, sir."

"H'mmm..." He seemed lost in thought. I wondered what was on his mind. This was obviously leading up to something.

"How would you like to begin training for space work?"

"Sir?"

"Outside the Station."

"Space work? Outside the Station? I—I didn't know there was any such work, sir."

He told me about it.

He told me about a whole kind of space work that I'd never known existed. And he told me I could be part of it.

Chapter 7

BIX WAS WAITING for me at the mess hall. I drew my quota of rations, and joined him in his booth. I hadn't even settled down, when Mark Atwood drifted over.

"Hey, Williams, what happened? You get tromped by Wilimczyk?"

Most of the food served on the Station is homegrown now; it comes out of the hydroponics section, which is also responsible for renewing our air. I munched a forkful of salad before replying.

"Nope," I said slowly. "It was just a little test."

"Yeah? And...?"

"I passed."

"Well, hey! Congratulations!" Somehow he was embarrassing me. I shrugged, and Bix and I exchanged looks.

"What kind of test?" Bix asked.

"Basically, sensitivity to different gravities."

"How'd he do that?" Mark asked before Bix could reply.

"An elevator—the officers' elevator; off limits to us'ns. He took me up and down and had me guess what level I was on." I didn't want to explain. I felt proud of what I'd done, but I didn't want to brag. I let him pull it out of me.

"Yeah? And you did it? Hey, wow! What'd you do? Figure out the intervals between levels?"

Suddenly I felt an active dislike for Mark Atwood—and not only Atwood, but all the other bright-eyed and bushy-tailed eager-beaver cadets who promoted their way through school, through jobs, through life. Always looking for the angle—for *their* angle—never trying to do what was actually wanted. Sharpies. If my life ever depended on a Mark Atwood, I might as well forget about it.

"Yeah," I told him. "I have a razor-sharp mind." I was putting him on. He didn't get it.

"Yeah? Well, that's great, Paul. That's really great!" I expected him to pound me on my back, but I guess the booth back prevented that.

"See you around," I said a little pointedly.

"Uhh, yeah, Paul. O.K." He nodded to Bix. "You too, Beiderbecke. Take it easy."

Take it easy. That was the Atwood Motto. Mark wasn't stupid—none of us were. But he was going to take it easy. Never volunteer. Let the other guy get the dirty work. Put in your time, and get out. He'd retire to a plushy job Earthside after his space service, and keep right on promoting the good things for Mark Atwood.

He left a bad taste in my mouth.

"That's not how you did it, of course," Bix said after Atwood had left. "Not after all the training you've been doing. How'd you score?"

"Pretty good. Nineteen out of twenty. I goofed the second one—I let Wilimczyk rattle me a little at first."

"Pretty good," Bix nodded. "So where's it get you?"

"I'm glad you asked me that, Dr. Beiderbecke."

He smiled and leaned back, steepling his hands on the table top in front of him. "Ah, so. Pliz to continue."

So I told him all about my interview with Commander Davidson.

"It seems we've been accumulating junk, up here in space, over the last twenty, thirty years. Old boosters, dead relay satellites, all that sort of thing. Official count has it there are over two thousand pieces of hardware floating around—and that's not counting what is known to have fallen back down. Of course we don't know how many the Russians have put up, either, but that must add a goodly number."

"Think of all the dead dogs," Bix added.

"Yeah. Well, not just dogs, either. We've recovered at least one manned satellite as well, or so I'm told. Ummm, formerly manned, that is."

"That's a bit grisly."

"The commander says that the Russians made at least five one-way manned shots into orbit back in the late fifties and early sixties."

"H'mmm. Maybe that explains the Russian observation group we've got up here."

"Really? Russians up here on the Station?"

"I bumped into them the other day. Four of them; two men and two women. Your friend, Dr. Cramer, was with them."

"I didn't know that. Well, anyway...It seems that all this space junk is just going to waste out there in orbit—especially since most of the orbits are slowly decaying, and eventually it will all end up falling into the atmosphere..."

"Where it will be transformed into falling stars," Bix said dreamily.

"Unless we recover it," I added.

"Thus thwarting poets and lovers the world over."

"Well, yes. But it would be nice from our point of view. Those things are all metal, and metal is what we need most on this Station."

It was very simple, really. We needed building materials to finish off the Station and for future construction jobs—like, for all I know, a starship: anything they want to build in orbit. O.K., most of this would have to be boosted up from Earth. There is a fair chance that we'll have working smelters on the Moon one of these days—

there's an experimental station there now——but in the meantime, it is ¢o$tly to shoot that raw mass up to us.

But some usable stuff was already up here, in orbit, its own function completed, scrap metal and ours for the taking. There were satellites the size of large basketballs, and booster sections forty feet long. It was all grist for our mills. It was all valuable.

Somebody had to go out and get it. Somebody had to ride a space tug out to each sighted piece of scrap, hook on to it, and tow it back.

Me. That would be *my* job.

"Your courses will be computed in advance, of course," the commander had told me. "And you'll have an onboard computer to handle course deviations and such details. Your job will be to ride out, make the hookup, and ride back. It's not a very glamorous or exciting job. But it is a job that requires specialized skills. And those seem to be skills you have."

It would mean working out in open space. That's what grabbed me. It would mean getting out of the Tin Can occasionally, and frankly, it would be a whole lot closer to my early dreams, as a kid, of being a Real Spaceman.

"I wonder if you see some of the implications in this job," Bix said thoughtfully.

"What do you mean?"

"You don't really like most of the guys up here, do you?"

"What kind of question is that?" I retorted.

"Look at the way Atwood bugged you. And he *likes* you, Paul—inasmuch as you'll let anyone like you. And you don't get along much better with the crewmen, either. Wilimczyk was just looking for a way to shut you up and put you in your place."

"Look, Bix, I didn't come up here to have one big party. I came up here to do a job, to *be* something. If there's something about me that rubs people the wrong way, well...they can just keep their distance from me. It won't bug me."

"Or—you'll keep your distance from them?"

"How's that?"

"In space, I mean. You're not likely to trip over Atwood or Wilimczyk out there."

"Oh, come *on*, Bix. There's a limit to this sort of analysis. Do you think I got this job to avoid people?"

"No, of course not. But I think you're pleased with it because it allows you to do just that. It takes the pressure off. You can function on your own, without worrying about the next guy and what he's thinking or feeling."

"Bix, I think you've got it backward. I don't dislike people *as people*. There are people on this Station for whom I have great admiration. On the other hand, there are those I'd be just as pleased to avoid. I don't think it's my responsibility to make friends with every goof-off up here. I was shipped up here because NASA has invested five years of time, effort, and money in me, and I am expected to pay off—to make good. And I am going to do exactly that. The less interference, the better.

"Which raises one other point. Look, Bix, I like you. You are not one of the goof-offs, and I think I'd have a fair amount of respect for you, no matter what the situation was. But you made me a pitch, back down on Earth. You said you were looking for someone you could loosen up with. You picked me.

"O.K. I went along with that. But here's the rub: You are putting me up tight. Maybe it's jollies for you to spend your free time running me through your little black box, but it most definitely does not unlax me. It has to cut both ways, Bix. Shake loose; stay loose. I need it too."

"Listen to yourself, Paul," Bix said. "Play that last bit back through your inner ear. Is that Paul Williams talking? Or is it a tough punk warning a rival off his turf?

"O.K., I'll level with you: I've been pushing you too hard. That's my fault. You're probably right—I see neat little psychological equations, and I tend to fit you into them. But let's not evade reality. You are a disturbed person, Paul. The more time I spend with you, the more I realize it. There is one whole aspect of your character that you are doing your level best to tromp on. Why?

"It preoccupies me, and you should take that as a compliment. Because I don't waste my time on people I don't have a lot of liking for either.

"But you know, the more I look back on those psych records of yours that I read, the less respect I have for Dr. Spittal. I don't think he had the vaguest idea of your real problems. He took all the measurements, and he fitted a neatly classified box around you, but he never really looked inside you. I have."

A muscle on his cheek was twitching as I stared at him. "What did you see?" I asked.

"I don't know," he replied slowly. "A lot of things that don't add up. Basically, I'd say you're alienated from people. You're very adept with *things*, objects. You're competent, and you take responsibility for yourself. But you shy away from situations that force you into contact with people. You deliberately bug people, if there's no other way you can escape them. You get snotty, very unlike your real self. I mean, like showing off. You're no show-off. Why the exhibition when we docked up here?"

"You really want to know?"

"Yes."

"You didn't see it, did you?"

"No; I was ahead of you."

"I panicked, Bix. I lost my sense of up and down, and I knew, when I started out of my seat, that I was falling head first. I panicked—tried to make a grab for something.

"I got lucky. I swapped head for toe. It was pure accident. Then I got myself under control, my training took over, and I was O.K. That snot, Edwards, thought I was putting on a big show to impress him. What could I do?" I shook my head. "Am I supposed to explain myself to every chowderhead who gets the wrong idea about me?"

"You know," Bix said with a bitterly admiring tone, "you really have all the answers."

"Coming from you," I said, "that's a laugh."

The first time I went out with Lee Hoffman.

He was a big, burly guy, and older than most of the crewmen I'd met. I found out he'd been a helicopter pilot down on Earth when he'd opted for NASA training. He was an old man, almost thirty-five. He had a ready smile, and a big, thick paw.

"You're the new space-hopper, are you? Good deal, kid. You'll like it or you'll hate it. This is the shakedown run. Then you'll be on your own."

The system had already been explained to me. Space Control down at Houston had plots on a lot of our debris; we had radar watch for whatever else could be found. Everything went through Houston computer-complex, and then was tight-beamed up to our own computers. Courses were calculated for whatever we happened to be in close proximity to, and fed into the onboard space-tug computer. We rode out and picked the junk up. It was simple—supposedly.

"Don't let anybody fool you, kid," Hoffman told me. "It's a lot more than a free ride. Lots of little problems come up. You'll see. We stay busy."

We were suited up and in the Station's core. Hoffman pulled himself easily up to the North Port.

"First thing to check," he said, pointing to a control box and dials. "Air. Make sure the cycle is through. If in doubt, run it through again." He demonstrated. He pushed a button. A red light came on and immediately winked off again. The opposite port of the air lock was closed. There was air in the lock. The dials said as much.

He spun a wheel on the port, and swung it open.

His helmet was still back on his shoulders. He pulled it forward and locked it into place, motioning to me to do the same. I did, and his voice sounded in my earphones, somehow much closer and more personal. "O.K., now we're on the air. They're monitoring us down in Control—right, Ben?"

Another voice chuckled, and said, "Check, Lee. Stay out of trouble."

"Now," Hoffman went on, "you're wondering why I bothered with this while we're still in breathable air. Good reason: Once you're not, it's too late. But mainly, it's a good habit never to forget being fully suited before going through this port."

"Has anyone ever, umm, forgotten?" I wondered out loud.

"Yup. I recall a cadet who was up here a couple years ago. He was on the same job you are. He came in here, dogged the port, readied his tug, and decompressed, all without his helmet. Not a pretty sight. After that, we made it a point to have everyone check out before entering the lock."

He turned and pushed through, grabbing onto something on the other side as he did. Immediately his body flew up and around, to the left.

"There're handgrabs as soon as you come through," he told me. "Get a hold on one soon's you can, to lose your spin."

I'd almost forgotten. The lock did not turn with the Station. Once I was through, he had the light on top his helmet on, and the bright light cut cleanly through the dark lock. I turned my own on, and—still holding tight with one hand—swung around.

The lock was large—a huge drum that served as far more than just an air lock. It was also the garage for the space tugs. These were the strange objects I'd seen in the gloom when I'd first docked. They were open frameworks of structural girders, designed solely for use in airless space. Up in front on each was an open console board and the hand controls. Immediately behind it was a single seat, just a flat bench, actually, without a back. The rest of the tug was fuel cells and batteries, fuel tanks and rocket engines. It had three big engines, and a number of smaller, maneuvering thrusters around the periphery. That was it. The tugs looked like desiccated skeletons, awkward and impossible to use. But I knew they were extremely efficient units.

Hoffman closed the port, and showed me how to fuel the tanks of one of the tugs.

Then he led me over to one side, and hauled out two AMU backpacks.

The Astronaut Maneuvering Unit is straight out of Buck Rogers. What it is, is a special rocket unit that straps to a man's back, and turns him into a personal space vehicle. It looks like a big, square box, with two small arms that fold out alongside you like the armrests of a chair. These contain the controls. The thing has its own air supply, fuel, tiny rocket thrusters, batteries, and running lights. It's a real delight. I wouldn't want to wear one anywhere where I weighed more than 1/50th G.

Lee helped me struggle into mine, and showed me how to connect the reserve air tanks to my suit's tanks. Then he slung his own on, in half the time, and thumbed the button that cycled the air out.

He told me to climb onto the seat of the tug he'd fueled.

"Where will you sit?" I asked. There was obviously room for only one on the seat.

"No problem. I'll just hook on behind you," he said. "Hook yourself in place."

Feeling clumsy, I fastened the small seat hooks to the loops on the thighs of my suit. There were some additional hooks on the seat board, and Hoffman clipped several short extension belts to these, and secured himself.

The tug was stacked among the others, and I wondered how he was going to move it to the outer port.

"If you were handling this, how would you get us out the door?" he asked me.

"Well, I was wondering about that," I confessed. "Since we're already hooked on, I guess I'd use the maneuvering thrusters."

"Right. First, however, we unlock the controls." He leaned over me and flipped a sturdy-looking switch. "Then we unlock ourselves from the dock." He threw another switch and a red light, which had winked on with the first switch, went off. Only green lights were on now.

"Hoffman to Control," he said. "All set. Am I programmed?"

"Control," said another voice, equally loud in my headphones. "Fully programmed and checked out. Everything's Go."

"O.K., kid. Take her on out," Hoffman said.

Me?

The controls were simple. They were quite like the smaller controls on my backpack: a direction control for my left hand, and an attitude control for my right.

I glanced over at the exit port. The huge door was fully open. Through it, I could see stars. They were fantastically sharp and bright.

Gently, I squeezed my left hand.

A bright torch momentarily flared off to my right. Then we were swinging out, around, facing toward the port.

I squeezed again, more gently.

Another flare, to my left, and we were halted, poised, pointed directly for the open port.

"You're doing fine," Hoffman's voice said, almost inside my head.

A forward nudge, this time.

And we were moving smoothly through the enclosed space of the air lock, out into the docking collar, and then—out into the vast enormity of free space!

Chapter 8

LET ME TELL you right now: This was it—this was the whole justification for my years of NASA training. They could cashier me out immediately, and I would not feel cheated. I'd known open space.

I was hanging over one of the most fantastic spectacles man will ever know. I felt like a trespasser. I felt as exhilarated as the first space-walker must have.

Below us, below the Station, half my view was filled by the globe of the Earth. We were hanging over it, and so close, so incredibly near, that weightless and "falling," I felt a moment's panicky thought that it could be only seconds before we would drop down into the planet's atmosphere. It seemed to hold and draw us, magnetically, just as it drew my hypnotized gaze.

Over half the Earth was in shadow, a black velvet that did not mask occasional glimmerings, whether man-made or atmospheric, I could not tell. One side, however, still held a thick crescent of light: richly blue, a stirred custard of clouds like icing on a vast cake.

Beyond the rim...I turned, and then my helmet no longer shielded me from the direct sight of the sun. Quickly the treated glass of my faceplate darkened, but not before I had spots before my eyes. I turned hastily away.

"Don't ever look directly at the sun," Hoffman said in my ear. "We have no atmospheric shielding up here; the ultraviolet is a lot more intense. It can leave permanent scars on your retinas."

I mumbled my assent, and stared out at the stars, above the darkened rim of Earth.

They were a rich profusion, a tapestry of subtle colors. I saw what I'd never seen before but only heard about: stars that were all the colors of the spectrum—blue, yellow, red, orange, green. Very few were actually white.

For a long moment I felt alone—totally alone—hanging naked in space. Then I pulled my thoughts together. I tugged my suit a little against the hooks, and felt the hard seat beneath me. Bright sunlight caught the edges of the tug's framework, throwing the girders into sharp relief. My arms and legs gleamed whitely in the sun; their shadows a dull silver that caught reflections.

Hoffman leaned over me and flipped another switch, cutting in the automatic control computer.

Instantly, small thrusters flared. We halted, pivoted, and half rolled to a new attitude. The Station was no longer at our backs, but above and to one side of us. Then the main rockets fired.

The acceleration was not great. It did not need to be. We were not pulling against gravity, and there was little inertia to be overcome. The rockets fired for perhaps twenty seconds, and were silent. The tug was vastly overpowered; it was designed as water-going tugs are: to handle loads many times greater than itself.

The next two hours Hoffman and I spent in quiet conversation, he telling me a little about his life on Earth, and how little it had meant to him, and giving me tips on how to handle the tug and about life aboard the Station in general. At one point, one of his observations on the mores of Station life drew chuckles from our monitor in Station Control, and Lee remarked, "Always remember, Paul, that life up here is a goldfish bowl. Everything you say when you're suited up is going to be overheard and taped by your Control monitor at the very least. And, for all we know, there are ears pitched to hear us Earthside as well."

"Really?" I asked. "I didn't think we were using that much power."

"You know those radio-telescopes they've got? Well, the stuff they pick up with those is pretty slight, compared with what we're broadcasting. And there are amateurs, down there—some sort of radio hams, I suppose—who make it a hobby to build really fantastically sensitive listening devices."

"What for?"

"For kicks, I guess. It gives them a jolt to eavesdrop on space operations. It's as though they had a little piece of it for themselves. Some of them have been at it for a long time, monitoring the telemetering instruments on the unmanned jobs we sent up twenty-five, thirty years ago. What can I say? Who can explain anyone's hobby?"

I saw it first, because I'd been watching more closely. It was a star—but a star that moved diagonally across the path of the other stars.

Then it was not a star. It was too close, too bright.

Our forward retros fired—a longer period, because these were smaller and less powerful—and still the bright object swelled before us.

It was tumbling, turning end for end in its perpetual orbit. It was a pencillike booster, thin, and marked with red letters on white.

"A military job," Hoffman remarked. "Tough boogies. A polar orbit we have to pull it out of."

I glanced at the control panel. The instruments showed we had a radar lock on the booster. The onboard computer fired side thrusters in short nudges, and suddenly we were alongside the long, cigar-shaped object.

"It's your show," Hoffman said. "I'm just here to watch."

I pulled the safety cable out on its reel, and hooked it to me. Then I unhooked myself from the tug. I gave myself a tentative nudge, and felt the tug fall away from under me. I reached out and grabbed a control arm, and my legs swung around until I was hanging upside down over the tug. "Don't laugh," I said. "I'll get the hang of it."

"I'm not laughing, Paul," Hoffman said quietly.

I followed the handgrips back along the sides of the tug until I was amidships, over the heavy cable lockers.

It took some work, me being weightless and having to keep a firm grip on something solid with one hand, but I got the lockers open, and pulled out the cables. These too were on heavy reels, and I had to unlock them before the cables would roll out freely.

The tug was no more than ten feet from the derelict booster, but the booster was slowly turning head for toe all the time. I could see it wasn't going to be a snap.

I pulled myself around until, both large cables hooked at my waist, I was crouching, with my feet firmly planted against the tug. Then I jumped.

I didn't put much kick into it. I wasn't trying to set a new broad-leap record. I pushed down slowly and smoothly, and equally slowly and smoothly, I shoved off into space.

My push would start the tug moving away from me, but not as fast. Of the two bodies reacting against each other, mine had the lesser mass and inertia. It didn't matter: I still had the cables.

I somersaulted before midpoint, so that I was heading feetfirst for the booster.

I missed. I'd thought I'd timed its tumbling action so that I'd touch near the center at just the right moment. Maybe it was the drag of the cables, but I'd miscalculated. I fell slowly past the booster not more than three feet above it.

"Use your backpack, Paul," came Hoffman's calmly reassuring voice. "But mind you keep the cables free."

I twisted myself about again, reaching behind me as I

did so for the control arms of the backpack.

Now in front of me, the booster gleamed almost blindingly in the sunlight. Three cables, two thick and one a light translucent Fibreglas, snaked back over it to the empty framework of the tug, beyond. Hoffman's suited figure gave me a wave.

The cables were still unreeling; I was still falling out, away from tug and booster.

I snapped the control arms down beside me, and fitted my hands over the knobby controls at the ends.

I fired brief bursts to halt my own tumbling, and line myself up properly. Then another burst, that started me back over my path again. The cables turned and followed me back, describing a 180-degree turn behind me.

This time I made fast to the booster. I made my way to one end, and the universe reeling drunkenly about me, fastened my cables securely.

The rest was anticlimax. I followed my personal, lightweight cable back to the tug, and hooked myself into place. A touch to the proper controls locked the towing cable reels, and started their rewind.

The computer did the rest. As the lines tightened, the booster, with its larger mass, tried to throw us into its tumbling path. The computer fired short blasts from the perimeter thrusters, and then the main rockets.

In short order we were heading back toward the Station, the now-quiescent booster clamped tightly to the tug.

"Very good," Hoffman said. "You did that in only twenty minutes; five minutes to spare."

"Sir?"

"The Station's not where we left it, you know. And we fell into a polar orbit to pick up the booster. We had five more minutes before the easy window closed, and we'd have been stuck with the hard one."

"The hard one?"

"Tricky maneuvering—heavy g's. A lot of trouble."

"I wish I'd known."

"I didn't figure you needed any extra worries. Don't

sweat it; I was standing by."

That sunk in after a while. Hoffman had been standing by, but I'd done the work. I'd done all the work. I glanced back over my shoulder: the huge cylinder of the booster was firmly in place, the cables drawing it snug against the cradle of the tug. A good piece of work. I felt moderately proud of myself.

When I got back, I headed for the mess hall. I was on a new schedule now, and I wouldn't be seeing as much of my fellow cadets, but on the other hand, I'd be better integrated into the regular social life of the Station—or so Bix assured me.

"That's what we're up here for, you know," he told me the night before. ("Night" is a fiction aboard the Station, but everyone follows. Actually, there are three shifts and eight-hour sleep periods are divided among them. But apparently the psychological effect of having a "night" and a "day" is important, so the lights dim from 9 P.M., Houston Space Time, till 5:30 A.M. We cadets were awarded the luxury of having our sleep period coincide with "night" time.) "We're not supposed to be a little ghetto of greenies. We have to mix, become part of the crew."

Nonetheless, I felt suddenly lonely. I hadn't realized how much I'd come to depend on the company of my fellow cadets—even those I thought I couldn't stand. But outside of those seven, whom aboard the Station did I know?

There were my instructors, Landis, Trimble, and Wilimczyk, but I liked none of them, and the feeling seemed to be reciprocal.

Among the others...I had developed a strong respect and admiration for Commander Davidson, but of course he was pretty close to unapproachable for a cadet like me. Lee Hoffman was a gruff man, but he seemed to have confidence in me, and I liked him. But there was a gulf separating us that I couldn't put my finger on. Age, I guessed.

That left the Cramers. And I hadn't seen them once to talk to since I'd come up.

My luck didn't improve much. I ate a lonely lunch and headed into the adjoining rec room, figuring I'd at least kill a little time watching TV. I was "on call" for space-tug missions, but Hoffman assured me that I wouldn't be called again that day. "Your next mission will be solo, Paul," he'd told me as we unsuited. "You did well on this one; you won't need me."

"How many guys are there on these missions?" I asked.

"Not many. There's Dean Ford, and Bob Tucker, and ... me, I guess. Tucker went down on the shuttle you came up on for two months' rotation. I guess you're his replacement for the time being."

"Is there that much work?"

"No. You'll probably get most of it. We all have other duties up here." His voice had lowered into a more confidential tone. "Most of the guys up here, they're earthlubbers really. They cope, they get their space leg. But most of 'em never get that real feeling for it. You've got it—it's a body awareness, an instinct, I guess." He clapped me on the shoulder. "Stick with it, kid. You've got what it takes."

I'd felt embarrassed for a moment, and then I'd looked up. He'd turned away. The back of his neck was red. He'd been as embarrassed as I was! For some reason, that was reassuring.

The rec room lights had been dimmed, and the big wall screen was full of glowing technicolor. They were beaming some Hollywood movie up to us. I slumped into a surprisingly comfortable lightweight chair, and took a look around.

There weren't many in the room, and at first I recognized no one. Then I saw Mary.

She was wearing a regulation jump suit, but on her it did not quite look regulation. I revised my opinion of her skinniness. She was sitting with a crewman. They seemed to be having their own personal conversation. I debated the merits of interrupting them, of trying to watch the movie, or just cutting out entirely.

I hadn't made my mind up when Mary solved it for me: she saw me.

"Hey, Paul! Come on over, Paul." She was smiling her usual bright smile.

I sauntered over and sprawled into a nearby chair. "You're not working?" I asked.

She made a face. "My first real breather in days. Daddy told me I'd been working so hard I should knock off for the afternoon. I haven't seen much of you, Paul. How are you doing? Oh! I'm sorry; I should've introduced you—this is Norm Edwards. He's the fellow who helped us at docking, remember?"

I hadn't recognized him in the dim light. He turned his head and nodded, and the light caught the sardonic lift of his eyebrow.

"Hello," I said evenly. "How's the gossip business?"

Edwards straightened. "Come again?"

"You've given me quite a little reputation, haven't you?" I said. I felt my temples throbbing, and I wondered why I was doing this.

"Paul, what are you talking about?" Mary asked. Her smile was gone.

"Hotshot here," Edwards answered her, "has a lot to teach us neos. He gives demonstrations."

"Why don't you get off my back, Edwards?" I said, my temper pulling a tight band around my chest.

"I didn't know you two knew each other so well," Mary said very coldly.

"It's obvious you don't know one of us that well," I replied. "This creep has been spreading stories about me all over the Station."

"You flatter yourself, Williams," Edwards said.

"He never even mentioned you to me, Paul," Mary said. "What is this all about?"

"Ask him, why don't you?"

"Don't you want to speak for yourself, Paul?"

"Why bother?" I replied. "I know when I'm outnumbered." I climbed to my feet and stalked quickly out of the rec room. I didn't look back.

I spent the next two hours in my bunk, playing the whole scene over in my mind again and again, trying to figure out where I'd soured it.

I'd blown the whole bit; I knew that. But *why?* Things had been going so well. I'd been pretty proud about my morning's work—why did I go out of my way to antagonize Mary by picking a fight in front of her?

When was I going to learn?

I was deep in a funk, when the door slid open, and Bix came in.

"Well, hey! How'd it go?"

"Lousy. Rotten. I blew it."

"What?"

I roused myself. "Oh, not the space work. That went O.K. It was afterward."

"What happened afterward?"

"Bix, what am I going to do with myself? I pulled off a fine space job, and impressed everybody. Then I went and scrubbed it all by shooting my mouth off."

"Tell me about it." He climbed up into his bunk.

I did.

"It's not as though I was deeply involved with this girl or anything," I said finally. "But she is a nice girl—a good person. And I acted like a Number One jerk in front of her."

"You care what she thinks of you?"

"Of course! Didn't I just say that?"

Bix made a few noncommittal noises.

"What about this Edwards guy? He was the guy who thought you were showing off, right?"

"Yeah. And I've heard the story from several different people. Every time I come up looking like a real obnoxious guy."

"And—?"

"And what?"

"Are you? An obnoxious guy, I mean."

"That's what I've been wondering," I said very quietly.

Chapter 9

LIFE WENT ON. If I was going to go through Dr. Beiderbecke's private psychoanalysis, I was going to have to do it on my own time. The next morning found me with a new mission: this time I would be on my own.

I was briefed at Control. Radar had picked up a sizable hunk of hardware on an eccentric orbit. It had apparently been out quite a lot farther. The orbit was now decaying, and the computer showed that this swing would likely be close to its last.

It was a routine run; they weren't about to hand me anything fancy for my first solo effort.

When I brought the tug out, the Earth was in full daylight below. Still in the shadow of the Station, I let the tug hang for several moments while I stared down over its side. Almost directly below was the Pacific. A little to the east was the cloud-shrouded coast of Venezuela. A few offshore islands were etched cleanly in a lighter turquoise against the aquamarine of the ocean.

It was all too big, too close. It felt as though it would engulf me—swallow me up. As a boy I'd thought of space work being a very different thing: jetting about through space with the nearby planets all no larger than the few coins in my pockets, and as flat-looking as the

Moon seen from Earth.

Below, the Earth was no disk. It was a huge globe that filled more than half my field of vision. There was no other way to think of it than as *down*. And, my senses told me, I was falling. As long as I worked out here, hovering over this great blue planet, I would always be falling.

I felt cold sweat on my brow, and lifted my hand to brush it away. My glove collided with my faceplate, and for a moment I was afraid I'd scratched it. Then my nose itched.

Resolutely, I punched the red button and threw the switch that put the tug on automatic, and let the thrust of the main rockets force the nervousness from my mind. I had a job to do.

"Do your job. Work is often the best therapy," Bix had told me the night before. "Do a good job and it speaks for itself. The people who count will judge you by your actions—not the stories they've heard about you."

"That's what I've been trying to do all along," I said morosely.

"Well, stick to it. What else can I say?"

"I thought you were going to run me through your little black box and make me your first successful case."

Bix's reply was a long time coming. "You know, sometimes I wonder if I'm really the hotshot shrink I pretend I am...."

Sheesh! Then we were both depressed.

Thrusters flared, and the tug's nose dropped. The on-board computer was making a few flight changes. I checked the instruments. We had a radar lock. I looked up and started a visual search.

It was pretty close before I saw it, and when I got closer I could see why. It had a low albedo; its surface had been painted a dull color that did not reflect much light.

The tug swung into a matching orbit alongside, and I

surveyed the object.

It was a capsule, and a large one. There were small viewports clustered around the nose, and Russian letters on its side. I'd hit a jackpot.

I went through my routine with the cables with a mounting sense of impatience—I wanted to look into that thing!—but with none the less careful discipline. This would be a big catch, and I wanted to make no mistakes with it.

I made the cables fast to my belt, and jumped over. This satellite had no tumbling motion to its orbit; it hung apparently motionless in space next to my tug.

I fixed the grapples first, securing the cables to the dead capsule. Then I crept to a viewport and stared in.

At first I saw nothing. The capsule turned from the slight spin I had induced upon hitting it, and one of the viewports opposite swung into the sun. A clean ray of brilliant sunshine cut through the gloomy interior of the capsule.

Two men and a woman stared up at me with dead and empty eyes.

I stared back for several moments in surprised horror, the hackles rising on my neck.

They were each strapped into couches. None of them wore space suits, but instead had on uniforms of some sort.

They had been dead for a long time.

Their bodies looked shrunken, aged, and wizened: mummified.

Dark skin stretched tight over grinning skulls. I could tell the woman from the men only by her long hair. For a moment I was afraid I was going to be sick.

"Hello, Control," I said weakly.

"Yeah, Williams. How's it going?"

"I've got a funny one here," I said. "A big capsule—Russian, I make it. By the looks of it, pretty old."

"Uh-oh. That means extra work for us and no scrap metal," Control said in my headphones.

"That's not the kicker," I said. "This one's not empty."

"*No?*"

"Three mummies."

There was a brief silence, a few clicks, and then a different voice. "Williams? This is Commander Davidson speaking. Bring that thing on in, *pronto*. Don't mess with it, and don't waste time. Get it back here, on the double! Got that?"

"Yessir!" I said. "Right away, sir."

I grabbed my life-cable, and yanked it to halt the free unreeling action. Then I pulled myself back along it to the tug.

Once reseated, I started the cable-winding motors, and pulled the tug up snug against the capsule. I'd had a wide window on this mission, and I knew there was plenty of margin for error, but the commander seemed to be in a particular hurry. Nonetheless, I wasn't skipping anything as I carefully checked out each detail for cradling the capsule, and reactivated the automatic control computer.

The computer "knew" that the tug would now have a much greater inertial mass, a new center of gravity, and an orbit that was dropping us closer to the surface of the blue world below us every minute. Almost instantaneously, it made its calculations, fired thrusters to change our attitude, and then ignited the main engines.

Hoffman met me at the docking port. "I'll take over, Paul."

I unhooked myself and used my backpack to jet me inside the air lock. There I braked, then turned and hung, watching.

Expertly, Hoffman took over the manual controls of the tug and deftly maneuvered it into the lock. They were taking no chances on this one. I felt cheated—done out, at the last minute, of the job which was my responsibility.

The outer port closed, and air cycled in. My suit relaxed as air pressure took over the job. Then the inner port was open, and men were hustling around me.

A hand gripped my arm. "Inside you go, kid," Hoffman told me, with a rueful grin. "This'n's too big for us chickens. You're off duty now. Scram." The grin took the bite out of his words.

I wasted as much time as I could in the mess hall and rec room, but no one showed up whom I knew—no one I could talk to. I wondered what was happening with the Russian space capsule, and what they'd found out about it. But if anyone knew, he wasn't telling me. Finally, after watching a couple of tired TV programs—why they bother channeling that slush up to us I'll never understand—I decided to knock off and sack out for a while. Sooner or later the news would be out. What I needed was patience.

Still, it burned me a little: the capsule had been my discovery, after all.

I told Bix as much when he dropped by.

"No, it wasn't," he said. "You were the first to get your hands on it, but Control had a radar pickup on it, after all."

"O.K., be a nitpicker," I said wearily. "The point's the same: I picked it up. I'm the one who told them about what it was. I could've kept my mouth shut about it, after all."

"Paul, knock it off. You did the right thing—you know that. Making the pickup—that was your job. Now it's in other hands, and they're just doing their jobs. Unlax."

"Yeah," I said. "You're right. As usual."

"Hey, Paul?"

"What?"

"Why aren't you out and doing things? I mean, like the way you did before—training yourself, getting your space legs, and all that?"

"I don't know. Depressed, I suppose. I tried to watch TV. First a situation comedy about a talking housefly that everybody's trying to swat—I wanted to myself! Then a news special about the spring fashions in Paris. It was just so much noise."

"That's not what I meant. You've stopped. I mean—

what's happened to that burning ambition to Get Ahead and learn new things?"

"Umm. Well, I *got* ahead."

"Paul."

"No, I mean it. You don't know what it's like, Bix, working out there. It's like swimming in a transparent, invisible sea. Down below is the Earth. You hang, suspended, over it. The visibility's fantastic. It looks impossibly close. And when you're coming back to the Station—did you know you can see the Tin Can twenty miles away? As if it wasn't half a mile. That's it, Bix. I'm here—I've arrived. Ambitious? I'd have to be nuts to be ambitious if it meant moving up to a job where I wouldn't get to go out like that.

"Besides, that's where my talents lie. That's what I was training for, only I didn't know it. I'm a space jockey, Bix. I'm the closest thing to a spaceman there is today. And I'm good at it, and getting better. Hoffman told me himself."

Bix sighed. "So when you're not out there, you're moping around watching TV, or bunking out in here. This is great?"

"What would *you* have me doing?"

"What'd I tell you the other day? Socialize, man. This is your chance. You're not a cadet any longer—you're a spaceman. You said it yourself."

I thumbed my chest, even though he couldn't see me from where he was sitting on his bunk. "I'm still wearing apprentice greens, fella. You forget that? To the rest of those guys, I'm just another greenie, and that's all I'll be."

Bix was swinging his legs back and forth rhythmically. His foot almost caught me in the ribs. "You gotta be kidding, Paul. Why, *I* know over half a dozen crewmen to talk to, and I'm still in training. I don't mean the instructors, either. I mean guys I've met hanging around and socializing. I've even been to a party. So look: maybe things seem pretty dull to you in here after you've been out there in open space, but don't palm it all off on how the big boys won't let the little boys play. That doesn't make it; not at all."

He jumped down from his bunk, whirled around, and faced me. "Let's put it in a concrete basis. Let's go hunt up some action."

"Now?"

"Right now."

"Aw, Bix, I'm tired."

"Come off it."

"Yeah, really. It takes a lot of nervous energy when you're out there, having to be completely aware of yourself."

"Come on."

"Besides, you didn't have to see three corpses staring up at you."

"Try it."

I shrugged. "O.K., Bix. Doctor's orders, huh?"

"My latest prescription: social therapy."

Several shifts were changing when we hit the rec room, and there were a lot of people standing around. I felt a little easier with Bix along—it was a comforting feeling to know that, come what may, they wouldn't *all* be ganging up on me—but there was still that knot of tension in my stomach.

"This is your next big challenge," Bix told me as we'd climbed down the shaftway. "Look at it as a new training period. Put some ambition into it."

Looking at it that way, I could see the sense in it, but it still had me very tensed up. I felt as though I was digging down through layers of personality I'd never known existed. I was tampering with myself on a level I'd buried and forgotten years ago.

And the strangest thing was, *I had no idea why I was feeling this way*.

"It's an anxiety reaction," Bix said, and we walked down the green corridor.

"Anxiety about *what?*" I asked.

"Well, that's a different question," Bix said sagely.

We stood near the entrance to the low-ceilinged room, pausing while I collected my nerve, and Bix sorted out the people, looking for those he knew.

It was a larger than average room. It was big enough so that you could see the curve of the floor, although that took looking for. At one side was the TV screen. At the moment it was mercifully blank. Lightweight chairs of aluminum and plastic were scattered about, and here and there a low table, on which stood empty and half-empty glasses. The bar at the far end was open, and after Bix had gotten the room pegged, we cut across to it.

We each got a Pepsi.

Clutching my glass in my hand, I did my best to survey the room in a totally casual manner.

Bix tugged at my arm. "Fellow I want you to meet," he said, pulling me with him.

A tall, blond man was standing and listening quietly to a shorter, more volatile man.

"So look, Dean," the shorter man was saying, punctuating his words with sharp gestures. "It figures that a goodly number of us semi-perms up here will get first crack at it, when they set up permanent operations on the Moon. The trick is to have experience and training that qualifies you."

Dean nodded. "So?"

"Special skills that relate solely to operating this Station are going to keep you here—they're less than useless elsewhere. You know that. And this Station—I give it ten more years before they abandon operations here."

"I've heard the argument before," Dean nodded. "I don't agree."

"Well, why? Why not?"

"Doesn't make sense," the big man replied tersely. "Sure, lots of things the Moon is better for. I figure we'll have a lot of heavy industry on the Moon in twenty, thirty years. But why use us? They'll ship up the men they need, directly from Earth. Men with industrial training. What do you know about smelting, Harlan?"

The shorter man snorted, and threw up his hands. "I need another drink," he said, and turned, walking almost directly into me. I stepped back quickly, but not before he'd bumped into me.

I was braced for another scene. He surprised me. "Sorry, fella; didn't see you," he said mildly, and cut around me while I was still mumbling my own apologies. I felt my face growing hot.

"Hey, Dean," Bix said. "I want you to meet a friend of mine, Paul Williams. Paul, this is Dean Grennell."

Grennell stuck out a big hand, and said, "Hyuh, Bix; Paul. Say...Williams...You the new space jockey?"

"Umm, yeah," I said. His grip was like iron. "I've uhh, gone out a couple of times." I felt myself starting to blurt, and closed my mouth firmly.

"Well, now. You're the man of the hour, aren'tcha?"

"Uhh, I am?"

"You brought in the latest prize—that Russky capsule?"

"Yeah. Most of the way, anyway."

Grennell leaned closer. "Tell me: is it true? Were there *people* in that thing?"

"More or less," I said. "They were well preserved."

"You didn't have a chance to tell me about that, Paul," Bix said, his tone curious.

"They were all dried up," I said. "They looked pretty awful."

"Mummies, I heard," Grennell said. "Hey, let's grab some chairs. I want to hear about this."

Fifteen minutes later I became aware of the fact that we had an audience. Half a dozen men were standing around, listening to me telling Dean and Bix about the capsule and what it'd looked like, and all of them seemed fascinated. Somebody had refilled my glass—still Pepsi—for me, and nobody was paying the slightest attention to the color of my jump suit.

It's not that hard, I told myself. *It's not nearly as hard as I thought.*

Chapter 10

"WHEN DO YOU figure they sent that thing up?" somebody was wondering.

"You said no space suits?"

"That's right," I replied. "So I guess it was after they were using air locks."

"That doesn't mean anything. All their manned flights were in ships with air locks," a man behind me said.

"They sure didn't worry about weight," Grennell agreed. "We're just lucky they didn't get to the Moon ahead of us."

"You can blame the world's weather for that," said a new voice. It was Mary. "Hi, Paul, Bix. Daddy says that if the jet streams hadn't changed and wiped out the Russian wheat crops four years in a row, we'd be the observers up here, and the Russians would be in charge."

She smiled at me as though nothing had ever happened—as though I hadn't been a complete jerk in front of her less than twenty-four hours ago. "Isn't it exciting?" she said, looking at me. "It's only the second manned ship we've ever found, and it's a lot more mysterious than the first."

"How do you mean?" I asked.

"What happened to the first?" Bix asked.

"What's so mysterious about it?" Dean asked.

She laughed. "One at a time; I can't keep up with you all. Well, first they found the one that had just a single man in it. That was three years ago, and that's when the Russian team came up as observers. That one was very simple. One of the guidance systems failed, and they couldn't get him down. He died when his air and food ran out." She shook her head. "It sounds pretty horrible, but at least they knew what was happening. They stayed in contact with him until the end."

"What about this one?" the short man, Harlan, asked.

"They've identified it. It went up in 1963."

"*That old?*" Grennell breathed.

"It's one of those they don't know what happened to. They lost radio contact with it right after it went up."

"What happened to it? Do they know now? Is your father working on it?" I leaned forward, excited by this new information.

"They—the Russians—looked it over, and they couldn't figure it out. So they called Daddy and some of the others in on it. I don't know too much; I tried to hang around, but Daddy told me to scoot. I suppose I'll find out by the time it comes to the reports and paper work. But of course then"—she dimpled, "then it'll all be classified and Top Secret, and I couldn't tell you boys anything. So I thought I'd better tell you what I knew, now, before it was too late."

From the reaction Mary was getting, I realized she knew most of the guys clustered around us pretty well already. That figured. I mean, after all: she's a reasonably pretty girl, and they're all healthy, normal men, and the male-female ratio on the Station isn't all that great. It still bothered me, though. Somehow it didn't seem right that she should be so friendly with all these guys.

"Well, hey," said a voice from behind me. It was familiar, and I tried to place it without craning my head around. I had a feeling it was somebody I disliked. "What's the story? What's going on? Hi, Mary."

Edwards. It had to be Norm Edwards. I felt myself tensing. Bix glanced up, over my head. Then he winked at me. *Keep cool*, I told myself. *Just stay cool*.

"Hi, Norm," Mary was saying. "Everybody's all excited about that new ship Paul brought in."

"Yeah?" He didn't seem to realize he was standing right over my left shoulder.

She told him about the Russky capsule again, and the strange circumstances under which it had originally been lost. "It was out of their line of sight too," she added. "They had to ask the British at Jodrell Bank to help search for it. But no one ever found out what happened to it. Until today, I mean."

"Well," Edwards sighed, "there's just one more problem for us."

Grennell looked up. "What do you mean, Norm?"

"That Williams kid. If he was a snotty type before, he'll be totally obnoxious now. Can you see him bragging up *his* discovery? Boy..." Edwards' voice trailed off slowly. Everyone had become very quiet.

I wondered what I was going to do. Everyone seemed to be waiting—waiting for me to say or do something. I felt a sick churning in my stomach.

Grennell broke the silence. "Now, Norm. Maybe you've got the wrong slant on Paul." He directed a depreciating smile over my head.

I heard my own voice responding from a great distance. "Well, Dean, you know how it is—once a show-off, always a show-off." I half turned in my chair. "Isn't that right, Edwards? Once a show-off, always a show-off? Isn't that what you always say?" I was at the wrong end of a telescope, and the world, the people, the room, were all impossibly tiny and far away. "Tell everybody what you think of me, Norm," I said. "Or—can we be buddies? Can I call you Abnorm?"

"Paul." Bix's voice was low but strong. "Ease off."

Edwards moved around me until we were facing.

"That's right, Williams. That's what I always say.

You've pegged it. 'Once a show-off, always a show-off.' O.K., you've had your say, little man. Now, blow."

I couldn't seem to hear anyone else saying anything, but the drumming of my pulse was loud in my ears. I felt very close to doing something wrong—something terribly wrong.

"Just a moment," Grennell's voice came to me over the roaring in my head. "You're out of line, Norm." Grennell, the Peace Maker, I thought bitterly to myself. Stumbling, I pushed my way to my feet.

"Edwards," I said very clearly and distinctly, "it would be a pleasure to cycle you through the air lock, *sans* suit." Then I turned my back and pushed through the crowd for the door. I almost tripped on the high door sill as I went through. My eyes were full of salt.

Bix followed me up to our room. He didn't say anything until we were both lying in our bunks.

"Why did you give up, Paul?" he asked. "As long as you kept your temper, you had him cornered. Everyone knew he was wrong. Hey! Remember back down on the Old Sod, when Krassner was trying to bug you, and you turned the tables on him? Why didn't you do it again?"

I had a headache. "I have a headache, Bix," I said. "I don't much feel like talking."

He was silent.

"You really want to know?" I said after a while.

"Yeah."

"I had to leave, to cut out," I said. "It was that or do something nasty. What I did to Krassner that day, that was nasty. He's hated me for it ever since. And we hardly knew each other before. That's a *kid* thing to do. I'm supposed to be older than that."

"Maybe you're right," Bix said. "Maybe so. As it was, you left Edwards to face the mob. Maybe it made good sense, tactically."

"Oh, tactically—!" I said. "I was ready to punch him one in the face, Bix. I was ready to blow everything, but good. I *had* to get out."

Another silence, while Bix digested that.

"What you said about Krassner," he said after a while. "I don't think he hates you. I think he looks up to you."

"Yeah?" I didn't believe it.

"Most of us guys do, one way or the other, you know," Bix said. "You're the silent, self-reliant type, you know. And you were the first to be promoted out of Instruction."

That took some thinking about.

Dr. Cramer summoned me a couple of hours later. I found him sitting in a cubicle office all but identical to the commander's. He was alone, and that was just as well. There was no room for a third person.

"Sit down, Paul. I wanted to talk to you about this capsule you picked up. I'd like your impressions of it. Oh, I know," he waved his hand, "you probably didn't see much of significance. This is a work break for me. I'm curious, and it's one way to relax and still be on the job."

"Well, sir," I said slowly, "I can't think of anything I would've seen that you people didn't."

"How'd it look when you first approached it?"

"Hard to see, sir. I mean, I've gotten used to seeing things better out here. There's nothing between you and what you're seeing, so the only thing that has any bearing is distance. But my tug's radar had a firm fix on the thing before I did. It was painted a nonreflective color, I think."

"Olive drab," Dr. Cramer remarked dryly.

"Yes. Well, so anyway, I didn't see it till I was almost on top of it. Then . . . well, it looked the way it does now."

"Not quite."

"Sir?"

"They've been cutting it apart and dissecting it, bit by bit. That's not my department, so I'm taking a vacation for the moment."

"Have they found anything yet?"

"Not really. Moscow sent up a tight-beamed video broadcast of the specs—not that they're that secret; the thing is long obsolete—and right now the engineers are trying to find what went wrong."

"What killed the people, sir?"

"That's a good question. There's still oxygen in the tanks, so that couldn't have been it. At first we thought, with such perfect mummification, there couldn't have been oxygen—they would've decomposed. But current thought has it that decomposition is largely a result of the work of microorganisms and parasites, insects and like that, and most of those were either missing from the environment of the capsule or killed along with the occupants. We do know that whatever killed them was sudden and unexpected, though."

"How do you know that, sir?"

Dr. Cramer flashed me a conspiratorial smile. "We're not supposed to spread the news yet, but . . . can you keep it to yourself for the time being? Even from my nosy daughter?"

"Mary?"

"There's nothing that girl delights in more than a secret to be shared. It seems to me we owe you something for reporting the find so promptly, and doing a good job of bringing it in, so—will you agree? Mum for now?"

"Umm, yessir."

"There was a log on board. The captain of the mission, Petrov, left a short, unfinished message. Roughly translated—and I'm quoting from memory anyway—it said, 'Radio dead, all instruments dead. Getting very cold. Headed on collision course with—' And there it breaks off. The handwriting was very irregular for the last several words."

"A collision course, sir? With what?"

Dr. Cramer sighed. "I wish I knew. There's no ambiguity in what the man wrote. Dr. Timkovsky, the head of the Russian group up here, was very certain of that. But that, of course, is less puzzling than the loss of radio contact, internal power, and heat. He may have been having delusions and hallucinations by then. The handwriting suggests it."

My mind remained with the first idea. "But, still—a collision course. He must've seen something. If there was something out there that...well, *attacked* the capsule...?"

"He had to be wrong at least on that point," Dr. Cramer said. "There was hardly a collision."

"That's true," I said. "I crawled all over the thing. There weren't even the marks of a near miss."

"So there we are," Dr. Cramer said. "All the signs of a genuine mystery. If this were a detective novel, all the clues would be there, and our hero—that's me, I guess—would come up with a tidy solution. I—"

A buzzer sounded, cutting him off. He clicked an intercom switch. "Cramer here."

"Doctor," said a voice with only a touch of accented heaviness to it. "It would appear that we are again in need of your presence...ah, your help. We have been checking the instruments, and—"

"I'll be right up," Dr. Cramer said. I guessed he didn't want to have me hear anymore. He nodded at me. "Thanks for dropping by, Williams. You'll remember our agreement?"

"Yessir." I was being politely dismissed. "Thank you, sir."

He looked up and grinned. "Don't worry. You'll hear all the rest from Mary or me before it's all done with."

My next surprise occurred on my return to my room. Bix was lounging around, a cat-ate-the-canary look on his face.

"Well, Paul, how went it?"

"O.K. He just wanted to find out how it looked to me, what I thought of the whole bit."

"You're really rising in the world. Dr. Cramer comes to you for your opinions...next thing it'll be the commander asking you to spell him during his next rotation to Earth."

"You look awfully smug about something, Bix. What gives?"

"Take a look in your drawer, fella. It's none of my business."

By now he had me thoroughly puzzled. This wasn't the Bix I thought I knew. I pulled the drawer open.

I'd divided the drawer into three sections: various non-clothing oddments, like a magic slate and a stylus; underwear; and my jump suits.

My green jump suits were gone. In their place were five *blue* jump suits. I picked up the top one. It was neatly folded, in the same way I'd kept my jump suits folded for the drawer. I shook it out.

Over the left breast was a small piece of cloth tape. On it was neatly spelled out: "PAUL WILLIAMS."

I looked up at Bix.

"You get to keep the green suit you're wearing now," he said with a grin. "A memento. The others they took away. I folded the new ones up for you. I liked that better than a pile of them on your bunk when you came in."

I shook my head. "They're really for me, huh?"

"Yup. No more greenie, you. You're In."

I looked up at him, suspicious for a moment of his tone. "Bix? This isn't another of your Dr. Beiderbecke ploys? You didn't promote these for me, did you?"

"Huh? You kidding? That kind of pull I haven't got. No, these came to you from the Powers Above. It's legit, Paul. You're a crewman now. Go shove that up Edwards' nose."

I sat down on my bunk, and stared at the jump suit in my hands. Blue. A symbol. For me, a symbol of acceptance. I'd been judged, and accepted. Now I'd not only be doing the work of a crewman—I'd *be* a crewman, and Cadet Williams no longer.

It brought tears to my eyes, tears I made no effort to brush away.

The next morning found me back on active duty, back at work. I had a Titan IIIC unit to pick up, and a tug to check out and service before I could make the pickup.

Yesterday's big catch was to be just another day's piece of work.

But this time I was wearing a blue jump suit under my space suit. This time I was acting as a full crewman.

I was very careful, very thorough, working over the tug.

Chapter 11

THE TITAN UNIT was down a lot closer to Earth—a good hundred miles lower. It was the lowest we'd scavenged. Lee Hoffman told me that scavenging operations had been going on at their present scale for only a few months. In fact, I was the first to be given full-time work at it. Now, of necessity, we were having to scavenge farther afield, into higher and lower orbits, and orbits increasingly removed from our own.

I was just fastening the grapples to the unit, when something made me pause, and look up. I saw nothing, but as I paused, a sudden stillness descended upon me.

At first I didn't place it. Then I did. My earphones—they were *dead*! The familiar, almost subliminally accepted hum of my radio contact with Station Control was broken. What did this mean?

I looked up again. Something was wrong—terribly wrong.

From the corners of my eyes, I sensed movement—up here, where there was no movement. Yet, I saw nothing.

There's an old quotation that Bix delights in throwing at me in inopportune moments. But it fit this one like a glove: "What was the curious thing, Dr. Watson, that the dog did in the night?" Sherlock Holmes's answer was, it did nothing. And *that* was the point of his suspicions. As Bix pointed out, every time he quoted the line, sometimes an *absence* is more suspicious than a *presence*.

I saw a little too *much* nothing. A section of stars about thirty degrees above the horizon of Earth was blotted out. It was a small section—maybe as large as a dime. But it was growing.

A chill passed over me—and then the thought, *Was that an actual temperature drop?*

Dr. Cramer's voice was loud in my memory as he quoted the words of a dead man: *"Radio dead, all instruments dead. Getting very cold..."*

Was it my imagination, or was I getting colder?

A shadow seemed to be blotting out the heavens. It was getting larger, growing in size, growing—closer?

Discretion is the better part of valor, I once heard said. With shaking fingers, I unhooked my lifeline to the tug.

I crouched against the Titan unit, and then jumped, kicking as hard as I could.

As I fell away, I somersaulted so that I could look back on the tug and the scrap booster. Had I done the right thing? And—had I done it in time?

The dark area was now the size of a half-dollar, and rapidly increasing in size. I could see nothing within the area, no glimmer of light. No reflection.

I'd kicked myself up, away from the booster unit, without really thinking about direction. But I was lucky. I was rising, on an upward parabola, away from Earth. I wondered if I should add the thrust of my backpack jets to that of my kick, but on a hunch I did not. I was receding from the unit and the tug at a good pace, anyway. I guessed I'd already traveled a quarter of a mile.

Then I saw it.

Or rather—I saw its silhouette. It had moved over the horizon line, and now it was gliding over the brilliant blues and greens of the planet below.

I could make out no details. It reflected no light; it was as black as the deepest space between the stars. Yet its outline revealed that it wasn't any stray asteroid, no errant chunk of rock. Its contours were irregular, and yet *created*.

That was what made my scalp tingle: the strange object below, still on an apparent collision course with my tug and the Titan unit, was a *made* object—*but not man-made*.

It seemed to have no symmetry, no obvious nose or tail, no apparent means of propulsion. It showed no flare of rockets, nor even an ion beam. It *moved*.

I said it wasn't man-made, and there were those, at first, who doubted me, who couldn't imagine such a snap judgment. They hadn't seen it.

It was alien.

It's the way a dog will always recognize another dog, Great Dane or tiny terrier, as a member of his species, but instinctively recognizes that cats are not. On a more sophisticated level, I had my own instinctual, intuitive awarenesses of how man-made things should *look*. Human beings think in particular ways that are, if only subconsciously, familiar to other human beings. We can sniff each other out.

This strange black object—it had an alien smell. I looked down on it, and I looked upon the product of thinking that was unhuman, unfamiliar.

They asked me, back when they were interrogating me and didn't believe me, how I could expect to recognize something that might be a startling new weapon from one of the Non-aligned Powers. I couldn't tell them then. I couldn't put it into words—any better than I can now. I can't tell you what that *thing* looked like; only what it did *not* look like.

It was not a rocket. It was not a cylinder, a cone, or a sphere. It was not square. It appeared strangely amorphous, full of complex curves, which I could only see by silhouette, their full complexity not suggested until the thing began to turn upon its longitudinal axis. (I have to resort to such a long-winded way of describing it, because the thing seemed not to have any ends, although I automatically thought of the front as being that which pointed the direction it was going. But that was at first, before it began rolling, and then eventually struck off on another course, with a new "front"...but I'm digressing, and I'm getting ahead of myself.)

Even its size was hard to judge. How far away is a two-dimensional object? With only its silhouette to judge by, I could not tell at first whether it was on my side of the tug or the other—whether it was bigger in size, and farther away, or smaller and closer. It wasn't until I had the two and their relative positions fixed in my mind that I could make an estimate.

I would guess and say that the thing appeared to be at least three times the size of my tug: sixty to a hundred feet on its longest dimension.

If its shape was not almost enough to bring a dog-snarl to my lips—a racial reaction against the *unknown*—there was also its color.

Black, as any science freshman can tell you, is not a color. It is an absence of color. Normally a given object absorbs most of the visible spectrum, reflecting only one color, or a simple combination of colors. If it reflects them all equally, it appears white. But if it absorbs them all, reflecting nothing, it appears black. No light returns to us.

Most "black" objects reflect some light, some color, especially in a strong light. The blackness is only relative. We've never learned to create a black so black that it absorbs the entire visible spectrum of light.

Somebody else had, though.

Hanging in space below me, its motion relative to my tug now all but ceased, orbits equalized, separated from the linked tug and Titan by no more than a few feet, the alien object was totally black. No light reflected from its surface. There was not the faintest glimmering—from it.

But then, suddenly, my tug began to glow.

At first the phosphorescence was too pale, against the bright backdrop of Earth, for me to catch it. Then the black satellite was below the tug, blocking the earthlight behind it, and I could see the strange glow clearly.

The tug almost seemed to be shedding sparks. I watched in fascinated horror. There was no doubt in my mind that what I was watching was exactly that which had occurred to the Russian capsule in 1963—over twenty years earlier.

I was conscious, too, of something else. I myself was surrounded by a pale-blue glow.

By this time I was well over a mile away from my tug; irrationally, I had thought myself safe, out of harm's way.

I was in direct sunlight. Freezing would be no problem. Just the reverse. And my suit power—the batteries that controlled my servomechs, metered my air, directed the thrust of my backpack jets—what was happening to it?

Cautiously, I touched my jet controls.

The kick of the jets, increasing the speed with which I was removing myself from the area of the alien satellite, was a welcome feeling. And I noticed also that the blue glow surrounding me was now flickering erratically, and beginning to disappear. It appeared that proximity to the thing below was what counted.

I returned my attention to the black marauder.

The tug was losing its halo. The sparklike discharge stopped. The alien object hung, unmoving, for a moment, and then turning on a different axis, began to move away.

I followed it with my eyes as it crossed over the bright planetscape below, until at last it had diminished to a black dot and was lost amid the confusion of surface details. It had taken a new tack, a different orbit. I wondered where it was going.

The tug itself was becoming hard to spot when I pulled myself out of my trance. I gave myself a mental shake, like a dog climbing to its feet.

My earphones were still dead. I played with my radio controls, but they were rudimentary; the thing was tuned to a single frequency. Nothing. I was not going to be able to make a report until I returned to the Station.

If I returned, that was.

The first step was to get back to my tug. I reversed my jets and brought myself to an apparent halt. It was hard to tell; there were no handy landmarks for reference purposes. I guessed by the feeling of acceleration: At first I felt the jets overcoming my inertial momentum in slowing me to a halt. Then they were starting me back. I realigned my course—in my higher, but not faster, orbit, I had been losing speed and stability, and was falling back, away from the tug below—and aimed my sight for where I'd last seen the tug, plus a little.

It took me over half an hour to get back to the tug, and I had gotten a little scared there. For some time I hadn't seemed to be getting closer, and I'd worried that I was not closing the gap with it. Then it was bigger, and closer, and suddenly I was almost upon it, and wasting fuel braking.

I'd aimed rather well; I wasn't but a hundred feet off.

The tug was dead, stone-cold dead.

It had no power.

It is not until you need it and it's not there that you realize just how important electricity is.

The computer, of course, depended upon it. But so did the thrusters. Electricity operated the remote controls for everything from ignition to metering of the fuel. Worse, the fuel pumps themselves, which feed the fuel into the thrusters, are electrically operated. The batteries were drained, totally discharged. Dead.

I toted it all up on the fingers of one hand.

First, I had no radio—no way to call for help.

Second, I had no computer—no source of navigation.

Third, I had no way to operate the tug—no vehicle for return.

Fourth, my air—a check of the dials showed that I had enough air for about five more hours—I was just lucky the backpack provided extra tanks.

Fifth—?

Things did not look good.

I'd hooked myself onto the seat board of the tug. I stared down through the open framework. I was hanging over Asia. Suddenly, I felt quite homesick—homesick even for a land and a people, still quite hostile toward us, whom I'd never known. Asia, China, India, Tibet—lands and legends from storybooks and history books: part of my vicarious childhood. I felt a hunger for the safety and security of Earth.

What could I do?

I had two courses of action.

The first, the most obvious, was that I should wait. I should sit here, and just wait. It would not take forever—I hoped—for them to decide I'd run into trouble and come running after me.

Of course, all they had to do was to arrive here any time more than five hours from now ...

I was scared. I was alone—more alone than I'd ever been in my whole life. I was alone, and helpless, in a totally hostile environment. Right now, riding through airless space on my dead tug, I was in the strong sunlight. The temperature "outside" was well above boiling. But once I entered Earth's shadow, it would drop to a minus 250 degrees. How had man ever dared to venture out into this terrible place?

The second course of action scared me even worse. I could try to return to the Station alone, with my backpack.

It was such a bold idea that it intrigued me as much as it frightened me. I tried to weigh the pros and cons.

On the minus side was the strongest argument: How would I ever find the Station? This wasn't a trip on the local subway. I would be dealing in thousands of unmapped and trackless miles.

Of course I was already traveling in an orbit with a velocity of several thousand miles an hour.

But if I guessed wrong—if I headed in the wrong direction, if I overshot—it would be a fatal mistake. While they might find me in time aboard the tug, they would never find me in the limitless reaches of space.

On the other hand, if I was successful, I would have accomplished a feat previously unheard of. The thought had its fascination, I'll admit it.

I checked my chronometer. I'd been out here for almost two hours, of which over an hour and a half had been spent in radio silence. If they had become worried by my silence, why hadn't they come after me already? If I tried returning, there was a slim chance of actually meeting my rescuers en route, unlikely as that sounds at first thought. More important, I just felt the need to be doing *something*.

It did not seem physically impossible to get back to the Station. It was in an orbit roughly paralleling that of the Titan unit, around a hundred miles higher. I had come down by using the braking rockets of my tug to slow my orbital velocity and drop me as Earth's gravity groped for me. To return, it was necessary only that I increase my orbital velocity by the same factor—and hope that the Station would still be in the same position, analogous to the Titan unit. If it wasn't, I'd never see it.

I was banking on one helpful factor: the Station's visibility. I'd remarked before that I'd sighted it from a distance of twenty miles. That gave me a twenty-mile radius of operations. I could do worse.

Of course, that required we remain in the sunlight, out of Earth's shadow. I wasn't sure how many hours it would be until we passed into the nightside.

I had enough fuel in my backpack for a fairly sustained use of the jets—say ten or fifteen minutes. With even a small thrust, you can build up a remarkable speed, accelerating over that period of time. I wondered if it would be enough.

I glanced at my chronometer again. Fifteen minutes had passed. The stars stared back at me, cold and steady, scant comfort, poor companions.

I stared down at the Earth, the planet upon which man was spawned and I had been born. It looked so close, yet so far away. How easy it would be just to go down...

The thought sucked me in for moments.... I could

desert the tug, and desert space as well. Space was cruel, inhospitable. I could fly back down, with my backpack, down into the air, down to Earth. Down to home.

I would, of course, be consumed in incandescence long before I touched ground. I would be entering the atmosphere at a speed that strips the heat shields from space capsules and shuttles, ion by ion, the friction creating an inferno of heat that would turn me into a cinder.

It was a good point to remember.

I looked up, searching for signs of a rescuing tug. I tried to pick out a stationary star against the moving backdrop of stars.

The sun crept into my helmet, its rays darkening my visor-plate. The stars disappeared.

I shook my head, and turned away from the sun.

I stared again at my chronometer. Three minutes, only, since I'd last looked.

I was sweating, and I felt a new throb, as a servomech discovered the fact when a drop of sweat touched an electrostatic grid and triggered the release of additional cooling oxygen into my suit.

My nose itched. It felt as if something was crawling up and across the bridge of my nose. Could a bug have gotten into my suit? I tried to focus my eyes, crossing them vainly, to see if there *was* something on my nose. I only made them ache.

Then I felt a hundred ants, crawling all over my body, working their way between my jump suit and my skin, across my shoulder blades and up my spine toward the base of my neck; up the inside of my left calf; under my right arm.

I felt hungry, and at the same time needed the facilities of a water closet. My skin was crawling, and I was beginning to approach a quiet hysteria: the prelude of panic.

I looked up again, shielding my visor from the sun with my hand.

At first I saw nothing. Then I saw it. A star! A star that

seemed to be keeping pace with me, as the others swept across the heavens.

Relief left me slumped on my seat board like a limp sack of grain.

But fifteen minutes later, I was tensed again. I shielded my face with my hand, and checked the "star's" progress.

It was still a faintly glimmering dot, high overhead. It had come no closer.

It took only about twenty minutes for a tug to drop down to this orbit, I knew. By now, it should've been very close; obviously close. *Why wasn't it?*

It took me another ten minutes to figure it out. What I'd sighted was not an approaching rescue tug, but the Tin Can itself. I had the Station within sight!

Chapter 12

I MADE UP MY MIND. I would try to get back alone.

I had only four and a half hours' air left. If I waited too much longer, I would be stuck; I would have no chance to save myself in the event that I was not rescued.

That faint star, not much more than a hundred miles overhead, was the Station: *home,* for me. I had it in sight, and that made my navigation infinitely more certain of success. What I needed now was to remember my math.

Although the Station was not much more than a hundred miles away, my journey to it would be one of several thousand miles. It was simple math.

There were solid reasons why I could not simply aim at the Station and let fire my jets. The first, and simplest, was that even if this was a bodies-at-rest problem, I'd never get there. That was one hundred miles *straight up*. I would be fighting Earth's not-inconsiderable gravity every step of the way. My backpack jets just didn't have the stuff to do it.

Even today's sophisticated rockets don't try to climb straight up. It could be done—*if* you had limitless amounts of fuel for it. You could climb up, out of Earth's atmosphere, at a steady five mph, if you wanted to, and had the power and the fuel to waste.

But instead we use speed: orbital speed. That takes us back to the ball on the string—centrifugal force. It is actually easier to climb into a shallow orbit and then increase your orbital speed to escape Earth's gravitational clutches than it is to climb straight up. Because when you increase your orbital speed—which is pretty easy, because you're traveling more or less *sideways* to the gravitational pull, rather than *against* it—centrifugal force throws you out, into a higher orbit. Your actual path is a spiral.

That was what I intended to do. I was going to climb *up* one hundred miles, roughly, by going *forward* several thousand miles—and by increasing my orbital speed as I did so. My path should then curve upward toward the Station's orbit.

The complications arose from the fact that, as I said, this was not a bodies-at-rest problem, but a two-bodies-in-motion problem. I had to time my pace so that when I arrived in the Station's orbit, I would not be too much ahead or behind the Station itself.

This I would have to do by actually jetting myself above or below the proper path of my spiraling orbit. As I figured it, a straight climb from increased orbital velocity would put me too far ahead of the Station. At midpoint, I would have to make a sighting on the Station, and then apply a correction that, while not decreasing my velocity, would push me *down* again, holding me back for the necessary amount of time for the Station to "catch up" with me.

Tricky? You better believe it. It would all have to be done line-of-sight, seat-of-my-pants. No instruments, no computers, to calculate the proper intervals of thrust. Just me: Paul Williams, whose brain is more complexly structured than any computer ever built, if somewhat less reliable. I would have to rely upon my intuitive abilities, my space legs—that natural "feel" for it that Hoffman had pointed out to me.

I checked again, to be sure. No rescue tug. I couldn't

help wondering, *why?* Why hadn't they *done* something by now?

But they hadn't. I was on my own. It was time I got started.

First I took off the backpack. I tied my tug's lifeline cable to it, to be safe, because it was necessary to check something. I had to have a look at my fuel gauges. I had to know exactly how much useful thrust I had left.

It's too bad they didn't think to put the fuel gauges out on the control arms, where a person could easily see them, but I suppose the figuring was supposed to be that you checked them when fueling up, before strapping the pack on. So I took the thing off and checked them.

I had about three-quarters fuel capacity. At full thrust, that was about sixteen minutes' worth; fifteen minutes and forty-some seconds, to be as exact as I cared to be. I didn't have a magic slate aboard to do my figuring on; I had to use my head.

I put the backpack on again, and unhooked from the tug. I crawled forward, over the dead control panel, until I was squatting against the nose. I measured with my eyes, seeking the true orbital plane (if that isn't a contradiction in terms), and then kicked off, jumping directly along it.

I was now slightly accelerating my orbital velocity, but not much. I opened up the thrusters.

I timed them, my eyes on my chronometer. I used a full eight minutes.

I turned to look behind me, once the thrusters were off again. I couldn't see the tug any longer; it and the Titan unit were lost to sight. I felt a pang of sadness; it was a mission uncompleted—a responsibility failed.

Then I glanced up at the faint star of the Station. It was no longer directly above, but somewhat behind. I would have to be extremely careful, I knew, in calculating the proper time at which to fire my thrusters again, to bring me within the Station's reach. A miscalculation of only minutes would mean my permanent exile, out here in open space.

A shiver passed over me. I felt naked and alone—terribly alone. I pulled my legs up under me, my knees against my chest, my arms around my legs, and tried to hug myself into a ball. I missed the tug already, useless as it was. It had been something solid under me, an object bigger than I was, to which I could transfer some feelings of security. It had been something real, something to hold on to.

I missed it.

It seemed to me that I had always missed *it:* that necessary something to hold on to. What was it Bix had called me once? *The cat that walks alone*. That was me, all right. The other guys looked up to me as a "self-reliant type." They should only have known how I envied them their safe dependencies upon families and friends.

Me, I'd never had many friends—I didn't make friends easily, and sooner or later I usually managed to alienate the ones I had—and my family, well...

Bix had asked me why I never went home.

Home. The word—the image—called up strange associations in my mind. *Home* for me was never like *home* for other kids. I knew; I watched TV, movies. I read books. I knew all the Great American Clichés. The red brick house with the white picket fence, flowers in the front yard, the sounds of children playing out back, and a friendly little dog yipping with pleasure as Pop comes home from work and a smiling Mom greets him at the door.

It must really exist, I guess. Even in my darkest, most paranoid moments, I've never thought the whole world was a sham—that everyone lived lives as empty and distorted as mine. I don't know whether I could even accept the idea, if it was actually true. But it isn't, of course. Other guys have doting families; the Mary Cramers of the world have their proud fathers. It's just me who's different.

I don't know when I first became aware of the difference. For the first five or six years of my life, I must've accepted it without quarrel. I don't know; I can't remember. But I must have, because I had no standard of comparison. I knew no one else outside my family.

My father objected to putting me in a school; I remember that. He wanted a tutor. We were living in Munich that year, and he didn't want me attending a German school and adopting German as my first language. I knew some German, of course—kids pick up languages very easily, and I was always bright at it—but English was always spoken within the house. My contact with the outside world was meager.

Mother knew of a private school, for American and English children. The classes were all in English, the snobs. She didn't think hiring a tutor was wise; it would be better to return to the States.

"Back to the States? Why?" My father's voice always held a vaguely petulant, whining note. "Just for the kid's education? We could ship him back, if that's what you want."

"And to whom would you suggest we send him? Your folks, or mine?"

"Now, that's an asinine question. You know quite well my folks are out of the question."

"Well, since you choose to put it that way, so are mine. You know they've never approved of you. If they got their hands on Paul, we'd never see him again."

"That's bad?"

"Roger!"

At that point they discovered I was listening, and put me back to bed. I spent three months in Mr. Bridgewood's School for English-speaking Children, in Munich.

That's where I found out about other children's families. I was driven to school each day by our cook's husband. Some of the other kids were chauffeured to school too, but most were brought by mothers or fathers.

Then there was the day someone asked me what my father did.

"I don't know. He's just my father."

"Well, silly, he has to *do* something. *My* father's a doctor!"

When I got home that evening, I asked my mother what my father did. "He drinks, mostly," my mother said tartly. I was fairly certain, even at that age, that this was not an answer to be used at school.

It took me a long time to find out what my father *did* do. We returned to Boston that winter, where we stayed for two school-free months in a hotel, while my parents feuded with my father's parents, and then we moved into a borrowed house in San Francisco, in which we stayed until we rented one across the bay in Berkeley, up in the hills.

It developed, from what I could overhear during my parents' low-pitched and intense conversations when they thought I wasn't around, in that hotel in Boston, that my father lived by clipping coupons. For a long time I thought that meant the sort of coupons you see in newspaper and magazine ads, or on cereal box tops. It struck me as fascinating and quite mysterious, especially since I'd never seen my father doing it. I wondered how one made a living (I'd learned about earning money then; in fact, I was voraciously reading all the recent paperback reissues of Horatio Alger I could get my hands on at the hotel lobby newsstand) out of coupons of that sort, and it wasn't until years later that I discovered that the coupons were stock-option coupons, and that my father lived on investments left in trust for him by his grandparents.

Those were the Swinging Sixties and Smashed Seventies—the era of the Jet Set, and the widespread use of psychedelic drugs. It was a period of violent transition, according to my history books—although from where I sit the Eighties haven't calmed down much, and things seem as much in transition as ever.

Put simply, my parents were part of the Jet Set. They were the Swingers of their era. And maybe it looked glamorous and wonderful from the outside—some of my later classmates thought so, anyway—but it wasn't. It was lousy.

It was waking up in the middle of the night to the blare of loud music, drunken laughter, and a haze of cigarette smoke that penetrated through three closed doors—probably via the central air-conditioning system—and made a nonsmoker out of me for life. It was the Morning After, when "Mommie has a headache, dear. Suppose you could find your own way around the kitchen?" and the living room area looked like a ruined battlefield—sometimes the furniture itself in pieces. It was low-pitched battles, usually on topics over my head, which broke off suddenly when I stepped into a room.

Mostly it was a mother and a father who were strangers to me.

I was eleven when they decided on a divorce. "You're old enough to accept the idea now, Paul," my mother told me. "We might've done it years ago, darling, but we felt you were too young. You needed a stable homelife."

I sure did. It's too bad they never provided one.

"We're going to be terribly civilized about it," she told me. "You'll stay with your father for half the year—during the summers, I think, when you're out of school—and with me the other half."

"But, Mother, that's not half and half. Summer is only a quarter of the year."

"Paul. Don't quibble with your mother. We can't have your schooling disturbed by hauling you all the way across the country every six months. Your father realizes that."

"Across the country?" I echoed.

"Your father is moving to New York. He has decided to take an apartment there. I'm sure he won't be without companions." Her mouth turned up in a bitter smile. "He never has been."

I didn't want to hear it; I didn't want to know about it. Already she was trying to make me choose sides.

It soon developed into a small war, earnestly fought by their lawyers. I was a pawn, a symbol, prized for its symbolic value, and nothing more. Neither of them really wanted me. Each wanted simply to keep the other from having me. I solved the whole problem for them by going to Space School.

If I've been self-reliant, it's been for a very simple reason: there's never been anyone else to rely upon. If I've been a loner, it's because I've always, as long as I can remember, been alone. Old habits die hard. Old patterns are hard to escape.

Home? Home was security I never had. Home was love I never received and never felt. Home was a word. I was a stranger in my own home.

Now, I sensed that my life was changing. I was beginning to develop a sense of security, of identification. I had a staunch friend, and the respect of people who mattered to me. *Home* was beginning to be a personal thing for me, a word with meaning, a place wherein I would fit.

Home was a tiny pinprick of light, hanging above and behind me, in cold and empty space, orbiting hundreds of miles above the Earth's surface, at thousands of miles an hour.

Home was a place I might never see again.

You're reading this; you know I lived to write it. So I can't pretend to a suspense that doesn't exist. Bix thought I should write all this down—not just My Adventure, but my whole, well, story of myself—as another kind of therapy. Self-revelation, he calls it, and he says that in writing about myself I should learn a great deal about myself. And I guess I have, to some extent. Of course, Bix's theories have a way of falling a bit short of reality; they're too tidy for real life, where nothing ever really gets tied up into a neat bundle and stamped *finished—cured*. Each of his ideas has a germ of value to it, and I'm grateful to him for each of them. His little "therapies" have done me a lot of good, when you total them up. But I think that even in sum, they were and are less important than the simple fact of his friendship—of his *caring* enough to try to make a "case" out of me for him to "cure." He's been like a brother to me, a brother I never had. *That's* why I'm most grateful to him.

But when you come right down to it, Bix furnished me impetus and confidence; encouragement and little more. The rest was up to me. It always is. Nobody else can make of you what you don't want to be. It was as Bix said to me that first night we talked. If you're a paranoid—and who isn't, in this age of depersonalization and alienation—nobody can work a cure on you until you decide you don't *want* to be a paranoid. Then, it doesn't take much help.

Me, I hadn't ever really tried to figure it out, but way down deep inside, I'd *wanted* to remain the way I was. It wasn't the most comfortable of lives, and it got me into trouble I didn't want sometimes, but it was *familiar*. It was my own rut of existence; it was comfortable. If Bix's therapies did anything for me, they prodded me from that rut. They made the rut a little less comfortable, and they made me a little more critically self-aware.

Basically, I didn't trust other people. I never had; I'd hardly been given any reason to. My mother would ignore me for weeks at a time, and then suddenly shower me with gifts I didn't want and a show of affection which I couldn't believe in and couldn't accept. My father was more consistent: he just ignored me. From the time I learned to read, my world was Books. I had devoured every book I could get my hands on, fiction and nonfiction alike. When I discovered that I could actually learn things in school, there was no stopping me. I lived in an intellectual world. You could trust *facts*. It was *people* you had to look out for.

I developed a shell of competency, of self-reliance. But inside, I was alone and afraid. I knew I was different. I knew I was missing something—missing out on a vital aspect of life.

Sometimes at night, while I waited for sleep to come, I would create monstrous fantasies about myself. They usually involved torture and ill-treatment at the hands of others. I was a Horatio Alger kid-hero, mistreated by everyone around him, yet somehow winning through. Sometimes I won through, and came back to either sneer at my former tormentors, or to forgive them in a burst of Christian magnanimity. On other, blacker occasions, I did not win through. I would lose an arm, or leg, or both, and haunt those who'd done it to me with their own shame.

The symbolism of it is obvious to me now, as I write this. I wanted to get back at my parents—shame them—for the way they had amputated a part of my life; my emotional security.

It was a sick kind of fantasying, and all the more terrible to me now for the way in which I then accepted its normalcy. A part of myself churned with self-pity. "They don't understand me; no one does," I told myself. It was easy to fall into the pattern of doing things that could be misinterpreted and held against me. "They don't understand me," I could say to myself, a familiar chant that always comforted me, and in so doing, reinforced the wall that formed my emotional prison. It was a lousy way to live, but it was *my* way of living. I clung to it.

You can do a lot of thinking when you are hurtling through space, hours between destinations, no chores to distract your preoccupations.

It wouldn't be true to say that in that long and fearful period after I launched myself into a higher orbit, my life actually passed before my eyes. But it did, in a sense, pass in review.

I realized that in what I was doing, I was gambling everything I had, on one roll of the dice. I was betting with my life. And that forced me to do some serious thinking about it. It forced me to realize that my life was too precious to throw away half used, tightly clenched within my shell of defenses, remaining a loner. I'd had tastes of what human companionship, friendship—and maybe even someday love—were, and could be like. As I hugged myself to myself up there, high in orbit over Mother

Earth, I realized that life was too precious a gift to waste as I had been wasting it. Living meant taking responsibilities for myself, sure—I had been doing that to some degree—but it also meant taking responsibilities for others as well. Bix, he was *concerned* about me. To that extent, he had assumed a certain responsibility for me. It was a lesson I needed to learn. I needed to learn to *care* about people.

I resolved that if I ever returned safely to the Station, it would be a lesson I *would* learn.

Chapter 13

I CHECKED MY CHRONOMETER. Two hours had passed.

I was taking the Slow Route; a tug, with its vastly greater thrusting power, could've made the trip half a dozen times. I had only my lightweight backpack jets.

And now it was time to use them again.

The dot of reflected sunlight that was the Station was far behind me. It took a careful search to pick it out against the dotted velvet backdrop of stars.

I angled myself until I was pointing down, toward Earth. The Pacific Ocean yawned invitingly below.

Again timing myself with my chronometer, I fired my thrusters.

Then I waited.

As I waited, watching the distant twinkle of the Station, I wondered. I wondered if I'd make it back, if I could pull the whole operation off. It was so chancy—so incredibly chancy...

I wondered, too, about the black satellite that had attacked and killed my tug. Where had it come from? Why was it here? Why was it preying upon our spacecraft?

If it was indeed the instrument of the Russian capsule's destruction, that meant it had been roaming over Earth for the last twenty-one years. That's a long time. Yet it had never been spotted before...or, had it? I thought about the mission we mysteriously lost in the late sixties, and I wondered if other tugs like mine had gone out on missions, never to return. What had happened? Had their mission Controls simply assumed a mistake on their parts—and a fiery plunge into Earth's atmosphere? Or had searches been conducted, and the dead men and their tugs found, enigmas as puzzling as the Russian capsule? How much hadn't we been told about the mysteries of space?

But I was letting my imagination run away with me. I was being paranoic. It was highly unlikely that there had been a series of previous losses to the black marauder. Once its presence was discovered, it would be hunted down and destroyed.

If it could be destroyed, that was.

I tried to think of the behavior characteristics of the craft. It could apparently move in any direction, abruptly, and almost at random. It appeared to zero in on any spacecraft in close proximity, and to suck the actual energy from it. Could this be its source of power?

But what was its purpose? *Why* did it do this?

That one I couldn't answer.

All right then; why hadn't it picked off more missions? Perhaps because space—even that globe of space within the immediate vicinity of Earth—was large. There was a fantastic volume of area to be covered. Did it sense other spacecraft from any real distance, or did it simply count on eventually crossing their orbits with its own? I favored the latter explanation; it made more sense, and explained why we'd seen so little of it.

When it had scooted off from the tug, it was following a new path, though. Was that deliberate, or at random?

These were questions I could only ask; I had no real answers. I tried to order my mind by grouping the questions logically, and setting up plausible answers, but my mind kept straying, back to a more elemental question:

Would I make it?

Fear would claw up through my guts, and then I would lay it to rest again by diverting my mind to thoughts of the marauder satellite, and my speculation over its origin and purpose.

Vainly.

My thoughts kept tumbling back, away from the abstract, and back to the subjectively real: *me*.

I tried to channel my thinking into a more constructive vein. Assume I *did* get back. Would I step into the old patterns?

Just what was my basic problem?

People—getting along with people.

Why?

It was like a session with Bix, with me supplying his questions as well as my own answers. I had to pry myself into a state of total honesty with myself. I had to solve these questions now, or admit defeat. This lone journey through space marked a turning point for me; I knew that. The remaining question was, would I take a turning for the better, or for the worse?

Why couldn't I get along with people?

The answer, Dr. Williams, is a simple one; you gave it yourself, only half an hour ago: you never had the chance.

Sure, blame it all on your parents, fella.

Well, *why not?* They didn't love me!

That's a handicap others have faced.

How?

By overcoming their early environmental pressures. By going out, beyond their defenses. By meeting other people, and by offering something of value to *them*.

Yeah? Buying their love?

You can't buy another's love. Nor friendship or respect. You earn it.

How?

It's the golden rule, fella; I thought you knew that. You give unto others that which you'd have them give unto you. You want others to care about you, you gotta care a little about *them*. Stop looking at other people as faceless enemies. Drop your guard occasionally. Get to know a few.

I do, of course.

Sure, and it's been pretty rewarding, hasn't it?

Well, yes...

How about the way you felt when you thought you'd goofed in taking Mary into that park? That was *real*, Paul-buddy. You were thinking about another human being; not just your own skin.

That's true...

And Bix. He bugs you sometimes, but what if he moved out of your room and left you to yourself?

I'd miss him.

Why?

He's somebody I can talk to; I know I'm not boring him. He digs what I'm saying.

He *cares*, right?

Umm, yeah.

Go thou and do likewise.

For a long time it had seemed the star I thought was the Station had not moved, and was no closer than ever. I blinked my eyes, and wondered if I'd lost it amid the real stars.

I checked my chronometer. I'd been out here about five and a half hours; I had only another hour and a half remaining.

Then, with a suddenness that was startling, the tiny pip of light began to swell, and I was horrifyingly afraid that in my miscalculations I would be passed by, the Tin Can hurtling past at something between one hundred and one thousand miles an hour. I clung to my control arms, the nails on my fingers all but tearing through the tough gloves of my suit.

Then, miraculously, I was hanging in space, not half a mile from the Station.

It was still moving overhead, but slowly now. I knew I could reach it.

I gave a quick touch to my jets to align me, and a longer blast to increase my velocity and lift me up directly into the Station's orbit.

The jets gave me a quick acceleration, but soon sputtered and quit.

I tested the controls again, gingerly. Nothing. The jets were dead. Their fuel was exhausted. Had I miscalculated somehow? I'd figured on another two minutes' worth yet.

The Station was growing closer every minute. I could see the sun screens of the solar power batteries cleanly etched by sunlight on the spinning barrel surface. The north pole—the docking station—was close overhead. I tried to figure my collision angles.

Not so good. I was not directly headed for my destination. Instead, continuing on my present course, figuring the movement of the Station, I would contact the north end somewhere near the rim.

That was no good. I couldn't tell if there were handholds, but even if there were, I would have a hard time grabbing onto one as it spun by, and the centrifugal force of the spin would probably throw me off again. Not so good at all.

I had to change my direction. I needed to be able to maneuver. I needed my jets.

I almost cried out of pure rage and frustration. *I was so close!* I'd lucked my way over the hardest part of the trip, and here I was within sight of home base.

And it was still beyond reach.

I felt like calling down the curses of all the gods of humanity upon this situation, and my rotten luck. Those jets—! The fuel gauge must've been inaccurate. It had cheated me, cheated me of those necessary drops of fuel which I so badly needed to complete my epic journey. I felt like tearing off the backpack, and throwing it as far away from me as I could, just for the pleasure of knowing it would briefly wink into flame as a falling star. I wanted to ruin my fists upon it, battering it, and me, into quiescent exhaustion.

Then my mind cleared a little.

The backpack—it had considerable mass. On Earth, it would weigh close to one hundred fifty pounds. It was compactly built, but it had a lot of weight built in.

When last on Earth, I'd weighed one hundred and seventy-five pounds. That was not so different from the mass weight of my backpack. If I took the backpack off, and threw it away from me, Newton's Second Law should give me quite a boost. If I picked the right vector for it, the opposite and nearly equal reaction should propel me in the direction I wanted!

But there was a drawback. Once I'd selected my course, and kicked away the backpack, that was it. There'd be no last-minute corrections possible. The only remaining items I could throw away were my exhausted air tanks.

My air tanks...

Maybe there was another way.

Fortunately, they'd had the sense to put my air gauges out on the control arms of the backpack, where I could see them. These gauges applied only to the tanks on the backpack, of course. The suit tanks had a direct connection. But I knew that the tanks were empty.

The backpack carried four compact, squared-off air tanks. My gauges showed two were empty. Of the two remaining, one was full and the other three quarters empty. That one was good for another fifteen minutes or so. I figured it would be long enough for my purposes.

The next problem was to get at the full tank.

I couldn't even see it, much less put my hands on it, with the backpack on. I would have to take the big thing off again. And time was not standing still. The Station was getting closer, and I could see more clearly that my present course would not take me to the docking port, or even close to it.

Sweat rolled down my face, partially clouding my face plate, as I struggled with close concentration to swing the backpack off without losing it.

I thought of combining operations: of kicking away the backpack, and then using the air tank for control. But granting I somehow made it, I could imagine what they'd say about losing a backpack. The things cost NASA about as much as *I* did. I'd save jettisoning the backpack for an emergency—if there could be any emergency greater than this one.

The air tank wasn't designed to be removed with gloves. The knurled screws were small and set almost flush. I lost a lot of sweat over them before the tank came loose.

Now I had it: my new jet. I set it in space, next to me, while I struggled the backpack back on. It traveled along with me; I picked it up again as though it had been on a shelf.

The Station was getting very close.

Angling the air tank around in front of me, I twisted open the valve.

A jet of highly pressurized air shot out of the nozzle. The tank kicked me in the stomach, and I almost lost it. It wanted to squirm out of my hands. Quickly, I cut the flow off.

Had it worked? I waited, and watched, clutching the tank firmly, my right hand on its valve.

Yes, I was swinging around, toward the docking port! I reaimed the tank, and gave a couple more quick blasts. The thing had a lot more power than I'd bargained on.

In moments, I was clutching the docking collar firmly with both hands. I was laughing, almost hysterically, and tears were rolling down my cheeks. I was still like that when they discovered me and took me in, minutes later.

They put me in the infirmary. I told them there was nothing wrong with me, and they told me I was still hysterical, and in a light state of shock. They took my blood pressure, my pulse, and tested my retinal reflexes. Then they gave me a couple of pills, and put me in a bunk, where I quickly drifted into a sleep that was close to oblivion.

* * *

O.K., you knew it all along. Dead men don't write books. You knew that I, Horatio Alger-like, would Win Through. You probably figured it out: with my native brilliance, and through NASA training, I was bound to come up with the right answers. O.K.; you knew.

I didn't. I didn't have the benefit of hindsight. I had absolutely no way of knowing whether I would succeed. It was touch-and-go right up to the last minute, for me. It was an elemental situation; one in which I'd struggled for my life, and not just my physical existence, but for a quality of meaning, for some understanding of who I was, and what I was here for.

I've set it down very imperfectly. I've mixed up a lot of my current observations with the ones I made then. It's hard to sort things out. When I look back on the thoughts that darted through my mind during that fantastic three or four hours, it is impossible for me to recount them without adding to them the thoughts they spark within me now: the additional insights and understandings that experience has brought me since.

So let me clear it up for you.

Bix tells me that while I was out there, hanging in space, waiting, I underwent what he says Jung calls "the dark night of the soul." This, as I understand it, is that time when one is stripped naked before one's own eyes, and an honest evaluation is forced. It usually occurs only during times of great stress. Bix says that in the book he read on the subject, many of the case histories involved men in times of war—real, front-line combat, where one's life was a very fragile thing and easily lost. He says that many apparent cases of heroic bravery are really cases of men undergoing this "dark night of the soul"—forced by desperation into saving their lives and those of their buddies by extreme heroism. A real confrontation, Bix says, with Death will change a man. He says it changed me. I agree.

Sometimes I look back on it all with a sort of dumb wonderment, and I wonder if my life could be so closely ordered by the Creator; whether, sensing that this was a time when I was ready for such a confrontation and Change, He did not bring it about for just that purpose. I dunno. Bix laughs when I mention the idea, and tells me I've gone a little nutty on the subject of mysticism. But then he admits that his favorite hero, Dr. Jung, was a bit of a mystic himself.

Naturally, my preoccupation with the salvation of my soul—if that is what it was—was of no concern to the Station personnel. And when they brought me in, I was not in condition to do much more than shudder and babble about my luck in getting back.

But the next day people came in to see me: Commander Davidson, Chief Staff Psychiatrist Speer, Dr. Cramer, and, quietly sitting back and taking notes in an incredibly fast shorthand, Mary. She had one of those magic slates that winds up like a scroll, and she used nearly all of it.

"Paul," Commander Davidson said, as soon as everyone had settled down, "yesterday, when you came back, there was a strong sentiment to have you shipped back down to Earth, on the first shuttle." He held up his hand to stifle my protest.

"Today," he continued, "you're a Hero, with a capital 'H.' We've recovered your tug, and it was pretty much as you'd said it was: powerless. Somehow, you accomplished a feat of navigation and space voyage that is still all but unimaginable. I'd like you to tell us, if you can, exactly what happened."

Chapter 14

I DON'T THINK they wanted to believe me, at first. Sure, something had happened to my radio and to the power batteries on the tug, but it would be a great deal more comfortable to believe in a freak accident.

I wouldn't let them.

"I'm sorry, sir," I said quietly. "It was definitely a spacecraft of some kind, and I am not imagining it."

"Ummm, Williams." It was Dr. Speer. "The human mind is capable of strange things when exposed to unusual stress. You were out there for five or six hours, totally cut off from your Station environment, your last link, the radio, severed.

"We've conducted tests—you may have heard of them—with volunteers who have allowed themselves to become environmentally isolated, in situations very much like yours: floating, all senses blanked out, totally dependent upon their inner selves. The results have been most interesting."

"I'm sure they have been," I said, a little coldly. "But I can't see that any of that applies to me. I was *not* environmentally isolated. My eyes were wide open, and I had full use of my body. I had things to do and to plan. It wasn't the same at all."

He had a bland, midwestern face, with small eyes and sandy hair. He blinked at me. "Young man, I believe I am more familiar with this sort of thing—"

"Excuse me, sir," I cut in. "Have you ever been outside the Station in nothing more than a spacesuit?"

"Why, no, I haven't, but—"

"Then I think you'll have to agree that you don't know what you're talking about at all." I was starting to get angry, and I paused, a little astonished at my temerity.

The commander coughed. "Ummm, Speer; I think the young man has a good point."

Speer opened his mouth, and then clamped it shut again. His eyes tracked back and forth between the commander and me. "Well," he said at last, "well, I can see this is not a situation in which I am needed." And with that he turned on his heel and went through the door. Unfortunately, his exit was somewhat spoiled by the fact that he had forgotten where he was. The infirmary was up on Level G, just inside the tan area, and he weighed something like a third of his Earth-normal. He bounded out, tripping over his feet, like a confused rabbit.

There was a short silence after his departure, which I broke with, "I guess I did it again."

Dr. Cramer laughed heartily. "Nonsense, Paul. That officious idiot has needed it for years. You've done us all a good turn."

I looked at the commander. His eyes twinkled as he nodded. Then he pulled the discussion back to the real topic at hand.

"I'm afraid that all this talk about whether or not you were imagining things ignores the central point: *something* put your radio out of commission and drained all the power from the tug. Occam's razor suggests that we accept your explanation. It is certainly no more difficult to accept than any other I can think of."

"Thank you, sir. I, umm...I wonder if I might ask a question, sir."

"Certainly."

"Why wasn't I picked up within half an hour after my radio went dead?"

Commander Davidson sighed and shook his head. "Sheer blundering, Williams; sheer bureaucratic blundering, and the most inexcusable sort. Your Control monitor forgot to log you out."

"Sir?"

"Eh? Oh, I forgot. You aren't familiar with the Control room procedures. We'll have to remedy that, of course. Normally when anyone goes out, and is being monitored, his Control monitor makes a record of it on the Orders of the Day record, which is kept posted. He logs it. He logs the time you go out, your mission, the computer-control index, and anything else pertinent to the mission.

"There's a good reason for this, and yesterday was the reason why. You went out about half an hour before a break in shift. Your monitor was scheduled to be replaced on that half hour.

"Now, had he properly logged you, his replacement would have been following you, and immediately caught on to the significance of your dead radio. But you *weren't* logged properly. Either no record was ever made, or some boob cleared the slate without checking, and erased you. We're looking into that. At any rate, it would appear that your radio went dead during the actual period of changeover, and went unnoticed. The new man in Control, having no notion you were out there, never thought to check for open but dead radio circuits. Indeed, it wasn't for several hours that you were missed. Then your mission supervisor, Crewman Hoffman, rang down to Control to find out what had happened to you; he'd just found out you weren't back yet. We immediately activated a radar search, found the tug with the Titan, and almost immediately thereafter, you, approaching the docking collar."

"Somebody goofed," I said quietly, a little bitterly.

The commander nodded. "Somebody goofed," he repeated soberly. "It's not the sort of thing I can excuse, nor will I make excuses to you. That you are lying here alive today is solely a tribute to your own bravery and skill, son. And we—all of us—are in your debt."

The commander left not long after, but his absence was filled by the presence of Dr. Yentov—Dr. Sonya Yentov.

Dr. Cramer introduced her; she was second in command of the Russian observation team, and in charge among them at present, since they alternated shifts and leadership.

Dr. Yentov was not at all what I expected of a Soviet scientist. She reminded me more of the women who used to do wild dances at my parents' parties.

Her long hair was a raven black, and her skin pale. Her eyes were large and dark, and her face soft and feminine. She could've gone to Hollywood and landed the lead in any TV series. She was in her early thirties, I was told later, but I don't believe it. She just didn't look that old.

She spoke with a soft voice, her English all but unaccented. She took my hand in the continental fashion, and told me, "You are a hero, Mr. Williams. The world will honor you."

The thought scared me stiff, and I blushed and muttered, "I hope not."

"However," she said, her eyes sparkling, "I am not here to tell you what everyone will be telling you. I am much more interested in that which you know. Tell me, please, all that you can about the black satellite."

I ran through it again, trying to recall every detail of what happened, trying to describe what was for me nearly indescribable. Finally, I took the slate from Mary, and sitting up, made a rough sketch of the thing.

"This doesn't really do it justice," I said. "The way I draw, it looks like a sponge." I laughed. "That's because everything I draw looks like a sponge." Dr. Yentov laughed politely.

"You realize, we cannot allow this thing to go on with its business," she said at last. She was talking more to Dr. Cramer than to me. "It is obviously the infernal device we must thank for the failure of the Petrov mission."

"Can you be certain?"

"Who can be certain?" She threw up her hands. "But how uncertain can we be without acting?"

"There's nothing to stop it from threatening us again," I added. I had no idea how prophetic that comment was to be.

Mary stayed after the other two left. She came over and sat on the side of my bed.

"I'm not going to tell you again what a hero you are," she said. "Pretty soon that'll be running out of your ears. But I am awfully proud of you." And without warning, and before I could dodge her, she was bending over me, planting a kiss on my lips.

We both blushed scarlet. Then grabbing her slate, she ran out of the room.

"So why should that bother you?" Bix said with a grin. "A pretty girl like Mary—half the Station is chasing her, and the only reason the other half isn't, is that the competition is too rough. They gave up. But you've had the inside track all along, fella."

I was back down in our room, staring at Bix's bunk overhead. I had on a fresh jump suit, and had a good meal inside me. I had just finished telling my story all over again, for Bix.

"I told you," I said. "I'm not ready to think about things like that yet."

"Things like what?"

"Aw, well, you know. Getting married and so on. My parents—I never told you anything about them. They, well, they had a pretty thin marriage, and they broke it up the year before I came to Space School. It—well, it wasn't the sort of thing I'd like to repeat."

"So, hey, Paul. Who said anything about marrying the girl? If you asked her, Mary would probably say the same thing—she's too young to be settling down to something like that yet. But that doesn't mean that she can't—I mean, that you two can't—well, she could still be your girl friend. You better think fast, old buddy. That's not just an ordinary girl, and odds are she knows it. She won't wait around forever for you to start paying attention to her; sooner or later she'll give up and pick somebody else. How about that Edwards guy, huh?"

"You convinced me," I said.

We were still sitting around talking, when there was a knock at the door. I was on the bottom bunk, so I was closer. I got up and slid the door open.

It was Bob Krassner.

He looked nervous about something, and I could smell him sweating about it. He picked nervously at a raw-looking pimple on his neck. The sight of him disgusted me.

"Uhh, Paul, I wonder if you could come down to the rec room with me for a moment?" He all but stuttered.

I couldn't figure it out. What did Krassner want me for? "Not right now, Krassner," I said. "I'm busy."

"What's he want?" said Bix.

"I dunno," I said.

"Paul? It's, umm, very important," Krassner said. He was shifting from one foot to the other.

"Why don't you see what he wants?" Bix suggested. He jumped down. "All right if I come along?" he asked Krassner.

"Oh, yeah. Sure, I meant to ask you."

So we followed Krassner down the shaftway to the S Level, and the rec room. And all the time I had no notion of what he was up to.

The rec room was dark when we entered it.

"Hey," I said, grabbing Krassner's arm as he started in. "What's going on?"

Instantly the lights came on.

I was surrounded by my fellow cadets, and a good number of the crewmen. Everyone was hoisting a glass, and all were raised toward me.

Krassner turned toward me, and the look on his face—the simple look of pure hero worship I saw there—destroyed forever the contempt with which I'd regarded him. "A—a little party, Paul. A surprise party."

Imagine! Those guys had set up a whole party for me. They'd wheedled a cake out of commissary, and had it decorated with "Welcome home, Spaceman!" in blue icing. They must've all dug pretty deeply into their pockets; everything was on the house that night. Several of the men had musical instruments, and they set up a little combo, the drummer improvising with an empty air tank, filling the room with cheerfully loud music. Most of the unattached women were there, too, and there was a lot of dancing.

What I liked best was that while the party was in my honor, they didn't make me the center of attraction. I don't think I could've sustained that kind of undiverted attention, and I'm grateful I didn't have to. Because this way, I could join in and have a good time.

Mary came in after a short while, too, and although I'd always been pretty shy about dancing with girls, I asked her if we could dance, and we did. I had to sit out the fast numbers, but on the slow ones, I did my half-learned basic two-step, one arm around Mary's waist, the other hand in hers, while she nimbly dodged my clumsy feet. We didn't talk much, but she had a radiant glow to her, and I found myself smiling and laughing much more freely than I ever had before.

There's a time when all things must come to an end, and the party was no exception. The shift was changing, and most of the guys had to leave, either for their rooms, and their eight hours in the sack, or for work. I found myself shaking hands with each guy as he left, and when it was Bob Krassner's turn, I was pumping his hand firmly and saying, "Thanks, Bob. This was really great. I mean it—thanks!" And I did mean it.

Then Mary and I were alone in one corner of the room.

It was suddenly quiet, and I found myself kneeding the knuckles of my left hand, and trying to think of something to say.

"Where do you suppose the Black Marauder came from, Paul?" Mary asked, breaking the awkward silence.

"The Black Marauder? Is that what they're calling it now?"

"Well," she giggled, "unofficially, at least. That's what I called it in my notes."

"It sounds like something right out of a science fiction story," I said.

"Isn't it? And don't tell me you don't read science fiction."

"I figured it would be more fun to live it," I said ruefully. *"Touché."*

"But, really—where do you think it could come from? Not another planet in this solar system, surely."

"No, I can't see that. We know there's no life to speak of on Mars, and nothing intelligent on Venus. They've got some crazy ideas about life on Jupiter, but it wouldn't be life as we know it—not the sort to make artifacts and build spacecraft. If it didn't come from Earth, it came from somewhere else entirely—somewhere outside our system."

"And you don't think it came from Earth?"

"No, I don't. I can't explain it, Mary. But if you ever see the thing, you'll know what I mean."

"It's kinda scarey to think about," she said slowly. "I mean, if you stop to think what it must mean."

"How do you figure it?"

"Well, for one thing it means that we're not alone in space. Others have been here before us. That really makes you stop and think, you know? It puts chills up my spine."

"I know what you mean," I said. "And it's not just that they've been here ... they've been watching us, and—*stopping* us."

"I wonder why."

"Perhaps they don't consider us fit to go about messing

up their universe."

"You got that out of a comic book."

"We haven't exactly eliminated war, yet."

"And neither have they—the Black Marauder people, I mean. Look what they've been doing to *us!*"

"Yeah. Plenty. And the way the thing works, you can't even get close to it, without being sucked dead. Boy, that's the perfect defense *and* offense."

"Oh, I don't know. I shouldn't think it would be that hard to disarm the thing—if they can ever find it again."

"How do you—"

"Hey, sorry to interrupt, Paul, but they need you upstairs." It was Lee Hoffman. "I thought I'd find you down here, Williams. Listen, the commander wants to talk to you. Get on over there right away, will you?"

"Where? His office? That's right around the corner."

"No, up in Control—Level Q. You know the way?"

I'd never been there, but I knew where it was. I said so long to Mary, and followed Lee up the shaftway. I wondered what they wanted now.

I looked around when I entered Control. It was not a large room, but it was crammed with equipment, floor to ceiling. On one wall was a bank of flat Sony screens. Some of them showing a relatively static scene of Earth below. Most of the others showed stars spinning past. Three were blank. I guessed those were the ones whose cameras pointed at the sun. Between them, they covered the entire periphery of the Station.

On another wall was a huge flat radar screen, flanked by smaller ones. Below was a large chart table, presently strewn with maps of plastic and real paper. The third wall housed a portion of the computer section, which I knew extended into the Computer Control, next door. There were keyboards and print-out machines. I saw no cards, no tape reels. Everything up here was the latest in hardware: sophisticated solid-state stuff.

There were several chairs in the center of the room.

Everyone rose when I entered. The group included Commander Davidson, Dr. Cramer, Dr. Yentov, and two others whom I did not know.

The commander wasted no time on preliminaries.

"Williams, you've gone through a real strain. How would you like to try it again? How would you like to go out into space and see your Black Marauder again?"

Chapter 15

LEE HOFFMAN and I would be going out together on this mission.

Based upon my sketchy description of its general direction, and of the time when I'd seen it, Houston's computer-directed radar had found the Black Marauder. They had narrowed it down, slowly, into a narrow quadrant of space, which they had divided and searched, painstakingly, until they had located—*something*. It did not return a proper echo at all, but showed as a phantom on their screens. They had at first dismissed it, but when it tracked perfectly, in a long elliptoid orbit, they agreed they'd found it. The data was tight-beamed up to the Station, and now our computers knew where the Marauder was too.

We had two tugs, tied together. I had the piloting job, while Lee stood behind me, as he'd done on my first mission—how many incredibly long days ago?

Our mission was a simple one: track down the Marauder, and then engage it.

The second tug was fitted out with elaborate recording devices, and a power source that emitted radiation on virtually every wavelength, including the visible spectrum. It also had solar power accumulators.

Our tug in turn was fitted out with a vast variety of telemetering devices, including a TV camera.

We approached the Marauder from above, so that its silhouette would be visible against the Earth below. When we had slid into a matching orbit at what we hoped was the safe distance of five miles, Lee disconnected himself from his position behind me, and began unfastening the second tug.

I twisted around in my seat to watch.

He worked with economy and precision, the sunlight picking out smooth sharp highlights on his suit and the framework of the tugs. It was almost like watching an animated line drawing, the contrasts between light and shadow were so vivid.

Then the second tug was free, drifting with us, but no longer tied to us. Lee gave himself a slight boost, and was up and at its controls. I watched him as he hunched over them for a moment, and jumped free, just as the big thrusters fired.

While he hung overhead, the now-empty tug gave a leap forward, like a startled cat, its computers in sole charge. Lee gave a couple of negligent blasts with his backpack jets, and then was drifting easily back down to our tug.

"Everything is Go," he said with quiet satisfaction. "Are you getting a good picture, Control?"

"Fine, Lee; just fine," came the reply. "We can't see Tug #2 yet, but you're zeroed right in on the, uh, Black Marauder."

"What do you think of it?" I asked.

"Hold on a moment. We're using the camera on #2 now, too. It's giving us a much closer picture...Hoo, boy! Would you look at that!"

"I can see it just fine from where I am, thanks," I said.

Tug #2 was dropping down closer, its framework a dark sketch over the blue radiance of Earth. Then—

"We've just lost contact with #2," said Control.

"Radio dead?"

"Everything—TV circuit, telemetry, everything. We're using you exclusively now."

Down below, the Black Marauder seemed to sense the object dropping down on it. It began that peculiar roll again, new bumps and protuberances rotating into and out of view, and then it started to rise, to meet the tug.

"Uh-oh," Lee said. "You think it's, umm, seen us?"

"I don't think so. I think it's got its mind on Tug #2."

"I hope you're right."

I was. The Marauder rose up, directly under the tug, cutting off the light that had outlined its empty framework, eclipsing it in effect, so that we could no longer see anything but the menacing bulk of the Marauder itself.

But then, a moment later, an eerie sparking discharge began to play around the tug's framework, and we could see it again, illumined by its halo.

"Would you pipe that . . . !" Hoffman breathed. "You can actually *see* it stealing the power!"

"I hope we're far enough back," I muttered. I looked for any faint halos on our own suits, but I saw nothing, and we still had radio contact with the Station. We were safely out of harm's way.

Below, the scene was drawing to a close. Great sparks seemed to be arcing off the tug. Then the halo slowly dimmed, and finally vanished.

The Black Marauder seemed to hang below the tug, motionless, for a breathlessly long moment, as though deliberating on its next course of action. Quite abruptly, it rolled on another, new axis, and flipped itself out and away from the tug on a new and different orbit. It vanished from our sight almost immediately.

"O.K., Tug #1. Go make the pickup, and get back here, on the double," came the orders from Control.

Was it my imagination, or did Control seem a little upset?

Control *was* upset.

We reported in immediately upon our return, and found

that not only Control, but the commander himself, was quite worried about something.

Mary told me about it, during a brief aside while the instruments we'd brought back were being analyzed.

"You know about the Mars Probe, don't you?"

"Sure." This was our manned probe to Mars. It wasn't to land on Mars, but simply to set up in orbit, take a lot of pictures, drop supplies for the next expedition (which was to make a landing), and return.

"Houston just told us that they'd reported seeing an alien artifact—Houston's words—orbiting Mars!"

"An alien artifact? You mean another Marauder?"

"The descriptions match up. They sent back a picture of it—it's in silhouette against Mars. The picture matches those we got of the Black Marauder!"

"What happened?"

"Nothing, really. They couldn't leave their own orbit to get closer, so they didn't get close enough to be captured by it. Houston's sent them word now to steer clear. They've got the thing's orbit calculated; it should be easy enough to avoid."

"If it stays put," I said doubtfully.

Instrument analysis was not as helpful as had been hoped—or perhaps it was *too* helpful.

Energy—*all* energy had been drained from the decoy tug. We'd had a minimax thermometer aboard—the kind that records the highest and lowest temperature of any given period. It recorded a temperature drop of over 450 degrees below zero. And that's all it *could* record.

"I'm amazed it didn't destroy the tug," I remarked afterward to Dr. Cramer.

"That's one of the puzzling things," he replied. "It did destroy some minor instruments, but most of those we'd put on #2 were recording instruments, designed to record up to the moment they ceased functioning, so that didn't matter too much. We expected them to stop. Still, I think only the fact that we built the tugs to withstand a temperature range of over 500 degrees saved them. More important is what this reveals."

"You mean about the way the Marauder drains energy, sir?"

"Yes. It appears to drain *all* energy, even the subatomic. It drains all radiation emissions, it drains the molecular energy, it—well, it takes everything. It's like a hungry blanket."

"Dr. Cramer," said the commander, coming up behind him, "I wonder if you'd care to go over these figures." There was something about the commander's manner; it was too carefully relaxed. He seemed to be under an intense strain.

Dr. Cramer made no effort to hide his own reaction. His jaw dropped, and his face whitened. "I—I take it there's no error?" he asked at last. I was momentarily forgotten.

"No error."

"Well, that makes things a little more imperative, doesn't it?"

"Sir?" I asked.

"Eh? Oh, Williams." He wore an abstracted look. He was quite far away. Then he seemed to remember where he was. "Paul," he said, "I'm afraid I'll have to ask you to forget what you just heard."

Forget what I'd heard? I'd heard nothing!

"Just what is it I'm to forget, sir?" I asked.

"I see no harm in telling him," the commander said. "I'm not sure it is wise to keep it a secret."

"Ummm, yes. I suppose not."

"Paul," Commander Davidson said, "this is a printout from our ballistic computer. It has calculated the new orbit of the Marauder for us." He paused. "By some remarkable stroke of coincidence, the Marauder's orbit intersects that of the Station. And when we checked our actual positions, we found that unless one or the other of us deviates from our present orbits, our actual paths will intersect in exactly sixteen hours."

• • •

They made the formal announcement a half hour later, over the Station's PA system.

There was no panic. We had fifteen and a half hours to think of something. At worst, everyone would suit up and evacuate the Station aboard the tugs. It was hoped there would be no loss of life. But the Station itself might well be irreparably damaged.

No one was certain of the Marauder's capacity. Could it suck all the energy from the Station as it had the vastly smaller capsules and tugs? Could we gamble on it *not* having that capacity? We couldn't.

We didn't have much choice, really. We would have to figure a way of dealing with the Black Marauder—there was no way we could move the Station in time.

Most groundhogs seem to assume that anything you put into space can subsequently be moved around pretty much to order. This just isn't so.

The Station was built to maintain a specific orbit. It *could* be moved, if we had to do it, but no one would guarantee that it wouldn't destroy the Station if the whole process of relocating didn't take a matter of weeks.

Look at it this way: you can't uproot a skyscraper and move it. The whole building is stress-engineered. Tip it two feet in any direction, and if it doesn't collapse on the spot, it would still knock the plaster off every wall in the building. The Station represented a huge and delicately balanced mass. It had been built while following a specific orbit, with a specific momentum implied in its orbital velocity.

Changing orbits would mean overcoming a vast inertial reluctance. If it wasn't done pretty much with kid gloves, the whole Station might just come apart at the seams.

To understand our feelings, you must understand that everyone aboard the Station was, in one sense or another, dedicated to it. We were the space people—the people who'd dreamed of space and the new frontier since early childhood. Most of us were nurtured on the science fiction of visionaries like Verne, Clarke, and Heinlein. We found ourselves dedicated to the vision of space exploration and conquest.

The Station was our beachhead. It was our first important outpost in space. It might not last long, as some thought, before giving way to other frontier fortresses, farther out, but it must live out its appointed time. To suffer a setback now might be calamitous—it might set our space program back by decades.

And yet, menacing as the news of the Black Marauder was, it was also thrilling. It confirmed one of mankind's deepest mingled fears and hopes: We were not alone. There were other intelligences in the universe, others capable of voyaging space. They appeared hostile, but...

"You know," Mary remarked to me as we ate an uneasy meal in the mess hall, "I'll bet those Marauders are nothing more than machines—and pretty limited machines too."

"What do you mean?"

"Well, do they seem intelligently directed to you?"

"No, not really."

"Look how blind they are. You have to come pretty close to one before it notices you. And then look at what it does. You were there both times. Wasn't the pattern identical?"

"It was," I said. "You're right. It was as though the thing was a machine with a set task. Every time it was triggered, it would go through the same motions, and carry out the same task."

"That's exactly what I meant," she said, and slid another forkful of food into her mouth.

"Hey, kids," said Bix, dropping down beside us. "Solving the Secrets of the Universe?"

"No, just of the Marauder," I said. "Mary's theory is that it's only a machine."

"Yes," Bix nodded. "That makes sense. It doesn't betray much intelligence or curiosity. It makes no attempt to communicate with us."

"Exactly what I meant," Mary said vigorously. "It wasn't designed to."

"I wonder what it *was* designed for," I mused. "Besides the obvious, I mean." I explained to Bix about the Marauder that had been sighted orbiting Mars. "It makes you wonder—is there one orbiting every planet in the system?"

"Yeah, and *why*?"

"I think the whole thing hinges on their age," Mary said.

"Their age?"

"Sure. We know that ours has been up here for over twenty years—but for *how much* over twenty years? It could've been centuries."

"That long?" I wondered.

"Why not? Suppose somebody came along, a few hundred years ago, took a look at Earth, and the wars we were fighting, and decided we were a menace to the Organized Universe. They put the Marauder up to keep us from contaminating space."

"Swell," said Bix. "Of course we got past it without much difficulty. But how does that explain the one around Mars?"

"Oh. I hadn't thought about that."

"Martians?" I said brightly.

"Come on," said Bix. "You know what the photos have shown: If Mars ever had any life on it—intelligent life, I mean—it's been gone for ages. There's nothing on that planet but craters and lichens."

"So maybe the Marauders are older than we think?"

"You know," Mary put in, "that might explain it!"

"Explain what?"

"Why they're so blind. Maybe they're so old that they're no longer working properly."

"Maybe," I said dubiously.

"Hi there!" Mark Atwood bounced over to us. "You guys figuring out ways to stop the Menace of the Black Marauder?" He spoke as though it was all one big joke. It took me a minute to recall my resolve not to be nasty to people anymore.

Then suddenly light dawned. A piece of memory turned over in my brain, and clicked into place. I spoke excitedly to Mary.

"Hey," I said, "back before they called me up to Control that time, we were talking, and, and you said something. You said you didn't think it would be hard to disarm the Marauder!"

Mary smiled, a very smug smile. "So?"

"So, *what is it*?"

"It's very simple. There has to be a limit to the amount of energy it can absorb. Overload it." Laughter glinted in her eyes. She had a secret.

"Overload it?" Atwood asked without comprehension. "How?"

"They've got all those big nuclear warheads over at the Military end," Bix said. "Is that what you were thinking of?"

Mary nodded.

"Well, look! We'd better go tell somebody," I said, starting to push my way to my feet.

Mary grabbed my hand. "It's O.K. I told my father about it forty minutes ago."

"You sneak!" I laughed. "You knew all along they'd be doing something."

"Yes," she said, "but I hope they don't destroy the thing. Think of what they could learn from it."

By now you, of course, are way ahead of me. If you didn't see the whole thing because you were on the wrong side of the world, you could hardly have missed seeing or hearing about it in the mass media. It was one of the biggest stories of the year.

Mary, Bix, and I wangled an invite from her father to see it all close-up. We got to go out to the observatory.

The observatory is in the south end of the Station, and like the north pole, it is gimbaled in such a way that it does not turn with the Station, and is gravity free. Most of it is a huge clear window—actually about ten separate panes of special glass, with a vacuum and an ionized field between each—and there is a remotely controlled telescope that projects outside the observatory, into open space itself.

The room is a large one, and ordered uniquely. Since there is no up and no down, seats have straps, and are placed wherever they are convenient to specific functions. This may put one seat upside down in relation to another ten feet away. There are handholds everywhere, all painted a bright green. We were specifically warned not to grab anything else but, because we might be upsetting some delicately adjusted instrument. In fact, we were just barely tolerated by the observation staff, and only Dr. Cramer's presence got us in. We tried to make ourselves as inconspicuous as possible.

Soon after we were in, they passed out goggles. These were, as near as I could tell, absolutely black.

"Can you see anything through these?" I asked Dr. Cramer in a whisper.

"You'll see as much as you'll care to," was his reply.

The Marauder was approaching us from above; its orbit went out in a wide swing. So the observatory was a perfect place to watch from.

But all the main staff would be down at Control, of course, where their monitors would provide as good a picture of what was happening, and with a great deal less danger. It was from Control that the missiles would be launched and triggered, and it was Control's instruments that would record the results and inform us of our failure or success.

The Military had groused mightily about it all. I hadn't seen any of that part of it, but Dr. Cramer, talking quietly to us as we waited, told us about it.

At first, the Military had not wanted to admit that it possessed any missiles at all, much less missiles with nuclear warheads. Commander Davidson had all but cracked heads together before they owned up to having a goodly storehouse full of the deadly things.

Then they had protested that they could not possibly, under any circumstances, allow the use of the missiles without a Presidential order. On this they were obstinate, and perhaps more justified. It *was* a heavy responsibility.

So Control had contacted Houston Control, by a tight-beam maser, and delicately suggested they get in touch with the President.

The President had been out yachting. It took two hours, while everyone bit his nails, before the Presidential Order was beamed back up to go ahead. It contained the necessary code passwords, and the Military were mollified.

Now, six missiles were readied at the docking port, and another six were being prepared. Each one had a fusion warhead: an H-bomb.

And it was about time.

Chapter 16

THEY SAY THAT the sun paled in the sky, beside the new sun. I don't know; I couldn't see them both. In fact, I could barely make out the flare of the hydrogen-reaction through my goggles anyway.

But that wasn't the first shot.

I felt quite cheated by the goggles. I saw nothing, and it wasn't until they did the tape replay on the lounge TV that I saw it. So in a sense I'm as much a bystander as you are; my knowledge is equally secondhand.

What happened was that they sent a missile out on a collision course with the Marauder. The warhead was designed to trigger mechanically when it was half a mile away.

We'd all been warned, and our goggles were on. What I saw was a brief lightening of the goggles' black lenses. That was all. On the TV rerun later, I got a better picture. The missile exploded, exactly as it was supposed to do. They slowed down the tape at that point, and we could see the globe of pure energy, the atomic reaction triggering the hydrogen fusion—the very process that goes on at the sun's core—expanding out into space.

Then suddenly it was snuffed out.

A black blot remained on the screen—the black

silhouette of the Marauder against the stars. It had leapt forward, until it was almost upon the site of the missile's explosion.

A second missile went out. This one almost triggered too late, and we could see, on the slowed-down replay, how the perfect globe of expanding energy was rapidly devoured by the Marauder. It was frightening.

But the third missile was different.

Again the globe of energy, again the blanket starting to snuff it out. Then a flare that was as bright as the sun.

It was all about eighty miles away. The Station's magnetic fields were supposedly an adequate shield against the radiation.

But we all underwent close examinations by the medical staff for the next two weeks, and I still get periodic checkups, aimed at making certain I am not suffering more subtle effects of the radiation.

That flare, at least, we could see through our goggles. It looked like a red and setting sun: bright, but not too bright.

"Oh," Mary cried. "They've destroyed it!"

We all thought so, but we were wrong.

Whoever it was—whatever race it was—that put that awesome machine in orbit around our planet is going to make a fearsome adversary for mankind someday. If ever we contact them. There are several schools of thought on that, and the one I subscribe to is that we will never meet them, although we may stumble, someday, across more of their artifacts.

We understand them a little better now. Not a lot better, but a little. And they have, inadvertently, immeasurably enriched us with their sciences, their techniques. I can't imagine that anyone among you has failed to feel some impact of the technological fallout of our discovery of the Marauder.

On the screen, after the radiance of the explosion had dissipated into space, we stared in awed astonishment at the surviving Marauder.

It was no longer black, but a kind of silvery golden, its rich and subtle, almost mindtwisting curves catching highlights from both the sun and the Earth below.

It had survived. Its defenses were gone (gone or just subdued?) but it, the Marauder itself, was whole, its surface apparently unharmed.

We'd known by then, of course. By then our men had gone out to the silent craft and forced their entrance, carefully opening (but not wantonly destroying) every circuit they could find aboard the thing. But still we gasped, and again I felt the tingle of confrontation—a confrontation with the mighty Unknown. This was a mightier work than man had ever known.

That's the story of the Black Marauder, of course. Our scientists are still picking its bones, still unraveling complexities that may take centuries to decipher. Dr. Cramer has had a field day with it.

We know a little more, now, about the Marauder. We know one essential fact that bears out my hunch about the likelihood of our meeting its makers.

We know that the Black Marauder—and presumably its companion orbiting Mars as well—is older than the history of Man.

They found sophisticated hunt and seek circuits, circuits which, if operable, would've allowed the Marauder to track down anything rising from or approaching Earth within its line of sight. Those circuits had failed, and they'd done so despite the fact that they were printed in a plasticlike substance with an alloy that should not decompose for millennia. But it had.

They're hypothesizing that the Black Marauder was originally only one of several satellites set in orbit around our planet to prevent any communication with other planets. In the many long centuries since then, the other marauder satellites have failed, and been lost, only this one still prowling our skies.

Why? Who so feared that space travel might come to

Earth, long before the dawn of Man? Did the marauder sentinels exist to guard Earth from outside exploitation, or to contain its inhabitants?

I'm afraid that's a question that will not be answered within my lifetime. The Martian marauder satellite may tell us more; it appears dormant, and with our new discoveries we may be able to block its energy-drain field anyway. But only time will tell.

But that's not the whole of my story. It can't be. I'm still young, still raw to space and life. I've not yet completed my mission here, and although Bix keeps telling me I'm a different person, it's a little hard sometimes for me to believe. Inside, I'm often a frightened boy.

Bix has been reading this as I've pounded out each page, night after night on my free time, keeping him awake in the process. He says that I should realize—and you should realize—that we've all got the embryos of the small children we once were, tucked away somewhere, inside our minds. We shouldn't ever really forget, he says. Life is a process of continuous change, of growth. But it's meaningless without comprehension, without continuity. We must remember where we have been, if we are to know where we are.

That's why I've written this: to tell me, and to remind me when necessary, of where I have been.

Now, I've got to finish. I have a date with Mary in the lounge, and I don't want to be late. I am not about to forfeit my rights to a girl I have found to be one of the most delightful of all creatures on Earth—or off it.

SCIENCE FICTION BESTSELLERS FROM BERKLEY

Frank Herbert

CHILDREN OF DUNE	(04075-5—$2.25)
DUNE	(03698-7—$2.25)
DUNE MESSIAH	(03940-7—$1.95)
THE GODMAKERS	(03919-6—$1.95)
THE ILLUSTRATED DUNE	(03891-2—$7.95)

Philip José Farmer

THE DARK DESIGN	(03831-9—$2.25)
THE FABULOUS RIVERBOAT	(03793-2—$1.75)
TO YOUR SCATTERED BODIES GO	(03744-4—$1.75)

* * * * * * *

BATTLESTAR GALACTICA (03958-7—$1.95)
   by Glen A. Larson and Robert Thurston

STRANGER IN A STRANGE LAND (03782-7—$2.25)
   by Robert A. Heinlein

Send for a list of all our books in print.

These books are available at your local bookstore, or send price indicated plus 30¢ for postage and handling. If more than four books are ordered, only $1.00 is necessary for postage. Allow three weeks for delivery. Send orders to:
   Berkley Book Mailing Service
   P.O. Box 690
   Rockville Centre, New York 11570

FANTASY FROM BERKLEY

Robert E. Howard

CONAN: THE HOUR OF THE DRAGON	(03608-1—$1.95)
CONAN: THE PEOPLE OF THE BLACK CIRCLE	(03609-X—$1.95)
CONAN: RED NAILS	(03610-3—$1.95)
MARCHERS OF VALHALLA	(03702-9—$1.95)
ALMURIC	(03483-6—$1.95)
SKULL-FACE	(03708-8—$1.95)
SON OF THE WHITE WOLF	(03710-X—$1.95)
SWORDS OF SHAHRAZAR	(03709-6—$1.95)
BLACK CANAAN	(03711-8—$1.95)

* * * * * * *

THE SWORDS TRILOGY by Michael Moorcock	(03468-2—$1.95)
THONGOR AND THE WIZARD OF LEMURIA by Lin Carter	(03435-6—$1.25)

Send for a list of all our books in print.

These books are available at your local bookstore, or send price indicated plus 30¢ for postage and handling. If more than four books are ordered, only $1.00 is necessary for postage. Allow three weeks for delivery. Send orders to:
Berkley Book Mailing Service
P.O. Box 690
Rockville Centre, New York 11570